REVIEWS FOR JUDITH ROLFS MYSTERY NOVELS

Bullet in the Night "A great whodunit! This book kept me entertained, intrigued and guessing all the way through. I admired the heroine for her grit and determination and smarts… There were lots of fascinating characters to spice up the plot. Every time I thought I knew who did it, there was a curve in the road." ★★★★★, Carlene

Directive 99 "A compelling story with an exciting resolution. I stayed up until 2 A.M. to finish." ★★★★★, Linda

Never Tomorrow "Just when I thought I had the plot figured out – I discovered I didn't. The characters were extremely well crafted and the setting of the story intriguing. The angst in my chest grew at each new development." ★★★★★, Victoria

The Windemere Affair "One of the most compelling and enjoyable mysteries I have read. The Lake Geneva locale setting provides an upbeat locale for this mystery. The ending was a surprise too. I definitely recommend this book. Rolfs' characters are likable, realistic and memorable." ★★★★★, Rebecca

MYSTERY AT WYCHAM MANOR

A NOVEL

JUDITH ROLFS

This book is a work of fiction. Names, characters, places and the incidents are the products of the authors imagination and/or are used fictitiously. Any similarities to actual people, organizations, and or events is purely coincidental.

Published by Fantastic Family Resources, Wisconsin.
Cover and interior design by Bojan.
Printed in the United States of America.

DEDICATION

To my husband Wayne,

Love you forever.

CHAPTER ONE

I met Zachary Taylor at a charity golf event on a fragrant June evening in Wisconsin. Spouses and plus ones had been invited for dinner and awards after golf in an enormous white outdoor tent. Not the formal type gathering, but a two-hundred-person buffet bash catered with simplicity and elegance.

I arrived slightly late, after making dinner for our three kids. Attracted by the sound of my husband Nick's rich baritone drifting from the hors d'oeuvres table, I immediately sauntered over. If his law practice ever slows, I tease him he can make his living as a radio announcer.

A six-foot tall, movie-star-handsome man was conversing with him.

Nick dipped a shrimp the size of a baby's fist in red, horseradish sauce. My man loves God, his family and sea food in that order. He turned and spotted me. "There you are, love." He pecked my lips. "Meet Zachary Taylor, my new golf buddy. He played in our foursome today."

"My pleasure." Zachary's hand shot out and closed around mine. His shake was warm and efficient. Lines around his eyes gave him a solemn, older-than-I-appear look.

I turned back to Nick. "How did your team do?" I'm a well-trained golfer's wife who knows to ask this important question first.

"We had fun, let's leave it at that." Nick grinned. "On a more pleasant subject, we were just talking about you."

I looked at him quizzically. "Well, I'm sure it wasn't about my less than stellar golf game."

Zachary's response was quick and gracious. "Do forgive me, Dr. Trevor, for being abrupt here, but I understand you're a professional counselor. I'd like to make an appointment. Do you have a business card with your number?"

So much for first acquaintance small talk.

"Sure, give me a minute." This wasn't the first time a social event had turned into a request for my services.

Nick knew the drill. "Why don't I leave you two a few moments to talk privately." He excused himself and headed to converse with a buddy across the room.

Zachary's eyes never left my face. "I'm leaving the country in a few days so I'm in a bind time-wise. Can I get in right away? I understand you're good at what you do."

"Well Zachary, this is not typical party conversation." I joked as I opened my purse and pulled out a card with a practiced reflex.

Zachary half smiled and slipped my card in his wallet without reading it. "I realize that. Sorry."

I went on high alert as I evaluated him. His words were smooth and easy as if asking a waiter for the dinner specials, but I sensed an intensity about him that was off putting. "Not sure if I should be flattered by your confidence in me or concerned." I sensed my eyebrows lift. "Why the rush?"

"It's a critical situation that I've already shared with Nick. Actually a pressing family matter."

He had to sense my hesitation. I chalked up my initial response to a nudge from the Holy Spirit. Then again, only the witch in Hansel and Gretel could deny the importance of family, America or apple pie. I bit my lip. Hopefully, I wouldn't come to regret my next words.

"Call my receptionist tomorrow. Tell her you talked with me and to get you in right away if possible."

"I really appreciate this."

I smiled. "I'm not always so obliging, but I have an hour reserved at the end of each day for clients in crisis or for catching up on paperwork. If none of my current caseload need that time, you can have it."

Zachary Taylor gave me a satisfied nod, wove his way toward Nick to say farewell and headed for the exit. I wasn't sure if I'd see him again. Fine by me, either way.

CHAPTER TWO

My renovated Victorian office building in downtown Lake Geneva is easy for clients to find. Fact is, I forgot about the previous evening's encounter with Zachary until he arrived early the next day for a four-thirty P.M. appointment. Sometimes new clients are no-shows. Not all are this eager, to be sure.

Ellen, my receptionist/office manager, leaves at four, so I handled Zachary's intake paperwork personally. To start I handed him a brown clipboard with insurance and preliminary history forms. My stationery logo reads "Comprehensive Counseling Services." Underneath in smaller print is "Individual, Marriage and Family Therapy."

This means I handle multiple issues and seldom know what to expect from one client to the next. My job is rarely boring, which I would detest, being high energy and creative myself. Plus I like helping people.

My strategy is simple. Solution-oriented, short term counseling. Brief review of past trauma, then primary focus on therapeutic change needed to improve the present situation. I attempt to apply tested scientific principles to the complexity of human relationships, but truthfully counseling is still a highly subjective process. We professionals dream otherwise.

While Zachary Taylor scribbled answers to the intake questions, I assessed him across my desk. A little too thin, Paul Newman's blue eyes and physical appeal. The tiniest patches of gray dabbed each temple. His fingers trembled when he filled out the presenting problem section on his form. Dressed expensively and tastefully, he wore the uniform of corporate America: navy suit, white shirt, standard fare except for the addition of color with a deep turquoise tie. This gentleman had pizzazz. No wedding ring, a watch probably worth more than a year's income in many countries.

Wordlessly Zachary handed me the completed forms. I scanned them quickly.

How I start a session with a new client varies depending on my initial observation of physical and emotional state. Zachary appeared tense.

"Let's get right to the pressing issue that brings you here."

His eyes held the shine of near tears when he looked up. Abruptly he turned away.

"I'm..." Zachary paused, organizing his words, like it was of maximum importance to express them in the right order. I waited.

"I'm divorced..." he offered, "I have a child er...a problem."

You and lots of people, I thought. Divorce is tough on kids. I waited.

"Actually, it's..." He tried again and halted.

Every counselor needs to be heavy on patience.

"A year after Laura Anne, my ex-wife, and I were married, she conceived." He sighed deeply. "Previously she'd assured me she was using birth control because we'd agreed to wait to start a family. Without my knowledge she'd taken herself off the pill. In retrospect, I think she wanted to know that she could have kids."

"How did you respond?"

"Fuming inside, but I tried to act pleased when she told me. I wasn't. Fact is I was scared to death. I didn't feel ready."

"Not uncommon for a new parent," I said empathetically.

"Well, unfortunately she sensed this and held it against me later, so I'm admitting how I reacted right up front." His look turned defensive. "By the time our daughter was born, I'd gotten comfortable with the idea, even excited about being a dad."

Zachary paused to look at his hands. I suspected he'd even become a diaper changer.

"Go on," I prodded.

I wouldn't comment until he'd finished, but Zachary obviously needed verbal encouragement to keep his words flowing. Clients can get lost in the emotional mire that springs from speaking long-unspoken thoughts. I'm sometimes the first person who hears the whole story. Friends get bits and pieces and take sides based on their vantage point. I get details too intimate for common knowledge as a safe outsider without a bias. It's the counselor's honor and privilege which I respect.

Zachary took a deep swallow. "About a year and a half after our daughter's birth, my wife decided she didn't want to be married to me any longer. She'd met an English Duke through her hospital volunteer work and intended to move overseas." Zachary shrugged. "Just like that she decided I was finished as husband and father. Inadequate and unnecessary. As a result, I haven't seen my daughter since she was eighteen-months-old."

I caught the flash of pain crossing over his eyes and knew he hadn't recovered.

"I'm so sorry. What a huge loss." I knew well how a life could be shattered as quickly as a piece of crystal. I'd observed way too many marital disasters.

I jotted down Zachary's time frame references on my yellow legal pad. "Adjusting to a situation such as this is very difficult. It would have been wise to come for counseling during your initial loss, but it's never too late. I'm glad you're starting therapy now."

"That's not why I'm here now."

I looked up, surprised, and made my "oh" sound like a question.

"I want to be part of my daughter's life. Laura Anne has shut me out completely. Fact is, I never legally surrendered my rights. Laura Anne just took off with our daughter assuming I would."

"What caused your desire for connection now?" I wasn't sure where this was going. "I mean why didn't you pursue legal custody arrangements sooner?"

"I know it sounds strange, but truthfully I was devastated initially by Laura Anne's departure, totally drained emotionally by the rejection I experienced from the divorce."

I nodded sympathetically and he went on.

"I knew I had failed as a husband and didn't feel capable of giving my daughter Ashley the care she needed. At first, I went along with my ex-wife's wishes, thinking a daughter needs to be with her mother. My daughter's older now and I, well, I've changed. I feel confident I can provide emotionally for my child, and I've always provided financially. Actually, in recent years my business has become successful beyond anything I ever dreamed."

"Have you seen your daughter during these intervening years?"

"That's part of the problem. I was supposed to have Ashley for four weeks every summer, but it's never happened. I've had no contact with my daughter since she was taken away seven and a half years ago."

I gulped. "You had no interest in pursuing a relationship until now?" I heard the surprise in my voice.

"Wanting to see Ashley? Of course I tried, repeatedly! Laura Anne won't even let me talk to her on the phone. She claims it would be upsetting to her. I send Ashley cards, presents and invitations to visit for her birthday and holidays. I don't even know if her mother gives them to her because Ashley never responds."

"How sad. Of course, it's possible Ashley may never have received your gifts or invites."

"Every spring, Laura Anne agrees to send Ashley to stay with me in the States for part of the summer, but something always interferes at the last minute. One year Ashley got chicken pox, another she broke her leg. Finally I've concluded my ex-wife is making up scenarios. You get the picture."

"Just to clarify, did you make an effort to go to England to see her? Did your business ever take you to Europe?"

"It wasn't necessary for me to travel internationally for work. As for going there uninvited, Laura Anne discouraged any visits."

"What's different now?"

"Six months ago I threatened to sue my wife for full custody if she didn't agree to give me at least half time with Ashley each year."

"Let me guess. Laura Anne refused to give you partial custody again?"

He nodded. "That's when I decided to take Laura Anne to court. I insisted legally on my rights. I figured she'd negotiate, but her response has taken me by surprise. Laura Anne has offered me full custody of our daughter with certain conditions."

"How extraordinary, but wonderful." I poised my pen mid-air and asked the obvious question. "What brought this about?"

"She said she and her husband Duke George will travel more now that's he's retiring and his responsibilities as duke have lightened."

"So suddenly, she's willing to change your arrangement? Quite an abrupt transition for your daughter and you?"

"Understandably a shocker. But a good one."

"And you have no idea how your daughter will respond?"

Zachary squirmed. "No. Ashley is presently in boarding school in England. For all I know my daughter may be completely unaware of this. Who knows what my ex-wife has told her about me."

"You mentioned stipulations." I shifted in my chair. "What are the conditions required by Laura Anne?"

"I'm to visit Ashley in England next week. First, we'll spend a day at the Duke's castle so Ashley can adjust to me, then take a short vacation excursion into Scotland with Laura Anne and Ashley. My ex-wife says she won't let me take my daughter unless she's confident that Ashley is comfortable with me."

"The question is how might she define 'comfortable'?" I shook my head from left to right. "Of course, you realize that her decision is very subjective. This gives your ex-wife a huge out. Still, I can understand why you're willing."

Zachary nodded. "I'm well aware of that, but it's my first real opportunity to have a relationship with my daughter. I will get to see her finally whatever the outcome."

"It's a risk acceptable only if you're emotionally ready if she backs out. Is being rejected again a concern?" I've learned over the years to never assume anything about a client's feelings. Talk everything through completely.

"No, but I want to make sure I do this right. That's why I'm here. I expect our connection might be awkward at first. It's important I get off to a good start." He paused and leaned forward in his chair. "I'd like you to travel with me and be present as my daughter and I develop our relationship the first few days."

I sensed my jaw drop open. Words failed me for a moment.

Zachary must have observed my reaction, but boldly went on. "I need to engage the professional services of your husband too, for on-site legal work. Laura Anne won't put anything in writing in advance. Nick said he could tie his travel in with an upcoming golf trip to Scotland, but only if you're agreeable. I want Nick present in case there's any last-minute issues."

I leaned back in my chair and inhaled deeply. "This is highly irregular."

"One more thing, I've done some research. I understand you have a daughter around Ashley's age. Having her join us could make my daughter more comfortable. I can make this an all-expense-paid holiday for the three of you. I know it's an unusual request, but I'll make it well worth your time."

Had I heard him correctly? I needed to process my thoughts. "Let me get this straight. We'll go with you overseas to help you through the initial stages of bonding with your daughter?"

"Yes. I'd be eternally grateful. I'll pay well for your time for one week and give a generous donation to your favorite charity also. I desperately want to make this work!" Zachary piled on more persuasion. "How about it?"

"Let's talk this through. From what you've said about your ex, I can see why you have concerns." I inhaled slowly. "Before I even consider this, I have a few questions. Zachary, you should be asking them too."

"Like?"

"Do you sincerely believe what your wife is telling you? I mean all of a sudden out of nowhere she's made this generous offer. Why?"

"I expect she took my lawsuit seriously. I told her I'd spend whatever it takes to see my daughter. I doubt that's how the Duke wants to use his fortune, and I imagine they'd like to avoid a scandal."

"That sounds reasonable."

"Then again, for all I know she's having an affair with some guy who doesn't want her child hanging around. Or maybe Laura Anne is worried I'll cause negative publicity for the royal family. Whatever her motive, I only care that I have a second chance to parent my daughter."

"Still, I find it bizarre that a loving mother would give up full custody. Do you have any messages regarding these arrangements from her in writing?"

"No." Zachary twisted the end of his tie. His face glowed with the anticipation of finally connecting with his child. I understood his emotion, but I had to ask the most difficult question.

"What guarantee do you have that Laura Anne won't change her mind on some trumped up technicality when you get there?"

"None whatsoever. As I said, I'm prepared to take that risk." Zachary shifted around in his chair. "I don't know, nor frankly do I care, about my ex-wife's motives. This is a chance for me to have contact with my daughter, and I intend to take it."

I nodded and murmured, "I see."

Zachary stared into my eyes. His features were charged with emotion. "I wonder if you do understand. Can you imagine how I feel every time I see a kid? The agony of knowing I have a living child who has never called me Dad or held my hand. At last I have at least a chance to be a father to my own child!" His face reddened.

"I can only imagine how difficult these years have been." I smiled sympathetically.

Zachary leaned back and sighed. "I'm in a position to devote my time and money to Ashley. I may marry again at some point. I've got my head on straight now and know I'm financially and emotionally capable of being a good dad."

"What about simply hiring a nanny to go to England and bring Ashley back? I could work with you and your daughter in the States as you build your relationship."

Zachary sighed. "No. Laura Anne insists on being present a couple days to be sure Ashley and I bond. That's why I need you there as a professional counselor to make sure our interactions go well and are documented by a third party. I want Laura Anne to have no legal excuse to back out."

I took a deep breath. "Okay, I'll consider it. As long as you realize Laura Anne could be simply toying with you and then say no in the end."

"This gives me a chance at least for my daughter to see the kind of man I really am. Who knows what her mother has told her about me?"

I leaned back in my chair and spoke my thoughts aloud. "I've handled the emotional aspects of custody switches before, though not in another country." I skimmed my calendar. "Actually, it would be possible for me to fit this in my schedule. And a trip to Europe in summer does sound attractive."

"Good! Jennifer, I need your answer as soon as possible." Zachary stood, reached into his pocket for a handkerchief and wiped his forehead. I guessed he could deal with being CEO of a huge corporation easier than relating to a nine-year-old child, but he could learn.

Zachary rattled off an unbelievable compensation plan for me and Nick, then suggested departure and return dates.

"Very generous."

"As I said, I don't care what this costs. I need a good counselor. When will I have your answer?"

"I'll discuss it with Nick and let you know tomorrow."

He shot me a quick smile, collected his briefcase and was gone.

After he left I leaned back in my chair. Wow! You've got chutzpah, Zachary; this is a creative solution, and you just may be able to pull this off. I jotted down session notes and slipped them into a file folder I titled "Zachary Taylor."

His problem didn't fit any of the pigeonholes I was used to. A quick check online for the guidelines on counseling through the Office of International Affairs assured me I could do consultation work with a client in another country. Truthfully, I'd never heard of another counselor taking on a client in such a position, but that didn't concern me. I'd been known to push the envelope before. If it was the legal thing to do, I didn't care about precedent.

Fact was the idea of a mini-vacation was enticing. I could certainly use one. I propped my elbows on my desk and took a fast mental trip through my own family's schedule during the next week. If I hadn't said "yes" to Zachary's 4:30 P.M. appointment tonight, I'd be home with them now.

Our daughter, nine-year-old Jenny, occasionally complained about my being gone so much. If I agreed to this trip, I'd definitely take her with. Our teen-agers, Tara and Collin were busy with sports and school. They wouldn't mind our absence. Plus my mother loved to stay at our home and fuss over them whenever she had the chance.

Another voice niggled at me. Jennifer, should you even consider this huge responsibility across the ocean in England? I prayed silently and felt a surge of peace. Like the runner Eric Liddell, I felt God's pleasure in performing the people-helping work I was trained for. Truth is I actually thrived on it.

Plus, this would give Nick and me a lovely vacation. Nick could indulge in his love of golf in Scotland for a few days. The thought of any serious danger ahead never crossed my mind.

CHAPTER THREE

The following Tuesday, Nick and I pulled out our suitcases and packed. Our travel agent said June in the United Kingdom could range from cool to warm. I selected a navy suit, jeans, two casual tops, and sweaters for layering. My cream-colored knit dress would work well with several colorful scarf options and gold jewelry to create different looks.

I filled one Pullman suitcase and a cosmetic carry-on. I'd long ago learned to streamline my travel wardrobe to one suitcase. Nick stuffed his large duffel with golf slacks and sweaters and planned to wear the one suit he was bringing. I packed another bag with Jenny's clothes.

At 8 P.M. Tuesday evening, the airport limo dropped Nick, Jenny and me off at O'Hare in Chicago. Zachary had booked direct flights for us to Heathrow.

I watched as Zachary pulled up in a silver BMW with a black-haired beauty, possibly of Indian heritage in the passenger seat. She hopped out on tall, slim legs and waited while Zachary grabbed his suitcase from the back seat. When Zachary returned the woman wrapped svelte arms around his neck and looked directly into his eyes for several seconds. Suddenly conscious of us looking on, Zachary kissed her quickly and removed her arms. She drew her gorgeous limbs back into the car, blew Zachary a kiss and drove off.

"Nice cabby," Nick joked to him as both their eyes fixed on the sleek woman in the vehicle vanishing into traffic.

Zachary didn't comment.

"Who's that?" I inquired. A counselor can ask personal questions others would consider too private. Plus do it in a nonchalant fashion and expect a response.

Zachary replied with a studied casualness as we walked into the airport. "Lydia. My business partner."

"Business?" Nick harrumphed.

Zachary turned red from his neck up, but recovered fast. It amazed me that a grown man could blush like a fifth grader when discussing a female friend. He said with refreshing transparency, "Actually it was Lydia's business at first. I went to work as a sales representative. Six months later I advanced to sales manager. Now I'm CEO and she's CFO."

"I'm impressed. Fast promotion!"

"I worked hard, get that straight." Zachary said a trifle testily. He obviously resented the implication that his move was based on issues other than competence.

"Don't get me wrong," Nick said, "I like it when God rewards effort."

"Things took off when the company needed some cash to expand. I'd saved up a few bucks and bought in as Lydia's partner. It helped that I had experience in the stock exchange and knew how to take the company public. We launched our IPO two years ago, got noticed by a couple investment magazines, and we were off."

"Sounds like an entrepreneur's dream," I said.

Zachary nodded. "We've been expanding exponentially ever since. Frankly, it's not a good time for me to be away. I'll need a few hours every day on my laptop to keep up. It's the only way I could leave."

My face froze. "I'm hoping you'll be giving priority to Ashley."

"Of course I will!" Zachary insisted. "You can stake your life on that."

"Okay. We'll work around your work responsibilities. Jenny will help entertain Ashley when you need to focus on them, won't you, precious?"

"Sure!"

I grinned. Enthusiasm is a strong part of Jenny's personality; after all, she is my daughter."

O'Hare Airport can be a traveler's horror, and today the international area was no domain of peace. None of us were frequent travelers. We waited more than half an hour in a snaking line until we were able to check our luggage efficiently. My precious, adaptable, nine-year-old

Jenny, normally not a clinger, stayed at my side midst the throngs of people without being reminded. A book to read, some stuffed animals for company and she's happy anywhere. I knew she'd settle in well on the plane.

People charged down the connecting corridors like worker ants in full swing. When we moved through the security checkpoint, Zachary set off a beep. A male member of the security staff took him aside and rapidly ran his hands like a slithering snake over Zachary's arms. He opened his coat, checked the inseams and flap, then directed his wand down Zachary's legs.

I paused to wait for him until a heavy-set, TSA security woman, hefty as a professional wrestler, urged me to keep moving. Still, I stalled a few seconds, looking back over my shoulder at Zachary.

Finally the guard let him move on.

When Zachary caught up to us, he had a frozen smile pasted on his face. "Whew! That's never happened to me when I travel stateside. Usually they say, 'Do you have any metal objects you missed like keys, etc. Take them out and pass through again.' I must look suspicious. I hope this isn't an omen."

"Good thing we don't believe in them," I said.

"Right. God's in control over the events of our lives, not superstition." Nick spoke matter-of-factly.

Zachary glanced at me. "You agree, right Jennifer?"

I smiled. "Absolutely. And I've committed our entire trip and its outcome into God's hands. You can pray for His guidance and protection as well, Zachary."

Nick responded. "Don't ask Jennifer about anything spiritual unless you have an hour."

I laughed. "Nick knows I can get highly verbal."

We followed bold black numbers to Gate 22. For the next hour, we occupied ourselves on our phones as we perched on hard vinyl seats waiting to board. I welcomed the time to decompress after our hectic day of preparation.

Finally, a loudspeaker announced priority boarding. "First class and small children, only."

"That's us." Zachary announced.

I picked up my briefcase and placed my hand briefly on Jenny's shoulder. "C'mon, sweetie."

We passed a flight attendant in a tailored suit wearing a felt hat and a perfectly molded smile. She pointed us to our section.

An attendant shoved our carry-on bags in the compartments overhead and snapped them shut.

I strategically asked Zachary to sit on the window seat next to me with Nick and Jenny across the aisle to my right. "No movie for me, but you go ahead, Nick. I need to confer with Zachary during the flight."

I gazed out the window and as usual wondered how this big chunk of metal could get off the earth much less fly across the Atlantic Ocean. Air travel always seems a miracle to me. I buckled my seat belt, then glanced out the window. Take-offs and landings give me goose prickles on my arms.

Nick placed ear buds in his ears. I reached across the aisle to hold his hand. I'm not afraid to die, but in case we go down, I like knowing we're connected. Think positive, Jennifer, I scolded myself.

After a smooth, efficient take-off, I turned to Zachary. "Okay, let's get started. First off, I know this is personal, but I noticed your business friend Lydia and you seem close. Sorry, but is it a serious relationship? It's helpful to know the family system I'm preparing Ashley to enter."

"Sure, I get it. Lydia and I had talked about getting married before this custody issue came up. We're waiting now because I'm not sure it would be wise or fair to either of us right now. What do you think?"

I appreciated that Zachary was transparent. This would make my job simpler.

Without waiting for my answer, he continued. "Right now, it's important to put my daughter's needs first. Don't you agree she'd be more secure if I wasn't sharing my affections with a new wife?"

"Lydia's relationship with you can be positive. It all depends on how we handle it."

"I don't know. It seems as if Ashley may have had enough of second-class status with George, Laura Anne's husband. That's my concern."

I paused a moment to adjust my seat. "What makes you think that?"

Zachary crossed his arms and leaned back. "I got the subtle impression from Laura Anne that Duke George didn't much like having a little girl around. That and the fact that she was sent off to boarding school at a young age."

I saw his point.

Jenny closed her book briefly to chat a bit. Leaning across Nick she asked, "What do you do for your work, Mr. Taylor?"

Zachary tensed. "I'm not sure how to best explain it to you."

Watching him respond to Jenny, it was obvious Zachary knew nothing about talking to kids. Being with Jenny on our trip over would give him some experience.

I jumped in. "He works with computers, honey." Every nine-year-old can relate to them.

Zachary smiled. "I sell software, educational programs and games. Would you like me to get some games for your computer at home?"

"That'd be great. Thank you!" Satisfied, her nose went back toward her book.

I was pleased to hear Jenny say thank you! I've threatened to implant earbuds with manners messages for my kids to hear during sleep, "Say thank you, cover your mouth when you cough, remember to say please, close your mouth when you chew."

I put thoughts of my sweet munchkin out of my mind and re-focused on Zachary's predicament.

"Do you mind a few more questions about your previous life with your ex-wife?" I asked.

Zachary looked sheepish. "If you think it's relevant now, although I admit it's rather an unpleasant topic. Laura Anne obviously wasn't a finisher."

"Interesting choice of words. What do you mean?"

"Simple. She could never finish what she began. A job, a marriage relationship, now she's giving up raising her child. Don't get me wrong, I'm glad of that and, to be fair, I know I did some things wrong in our marriage. I can't put all the blame on Laura Anne."

"Of course, the marriage dynamic is created by two. I'm not going to beat you up over anything. Dredging up old wounds may hurt a bit, but I don't want any surprises from the past destroying a happy future with your daughter."

The flight attendant rolled her cart up the aisle and stopped at our row to offer drinks. Zachary and I ordered ginger ales. "No ice for me, thanks." I waited while she served us, and we settled the glasses on our trays.

"Now when did the affair with Laura Anne and Duke George begin?" I asked.

Zachary flinched. "About four years into our marriage, Laura Anne met the Duke of Wycham, when he came to the States for an eye operation by a renown surgeon in Chicago. At the time Laura Anne was spending two mornings a week as a volunteer at the hospital—more for social status than to serve patients in my personal opinion.

She spent time with George, the Duke of Wycham, during his recuperation, brought newspapers around, that sort of thing. Read to him while his eyes were patched. In gratitude, supposedly, he invited her to England for a weekend. She stayed two weeks. Next thing I knew, she came back to announce our divorce, get Ashley and ship all her belongings."

"That was fast."

"Of course! Laura Anne was impressed. He was rich. We were poor. My prospects at the time weren't looking good despite the fact that I put in long days at work, probably left her alone too much." He shrugged.

"How was the Duke's overall health?"

Zachary looked at me sharply, probably knew where I was going with this.

"Are you asking was Laura Anne a gold digger eager to line up an inheritance from an elderly sick man? I don't think so. Duke George recovered quickly and was released from the hospital. He'll probably outlive me although he's seventeen years older than Laura Anne."

"You mentioned things you did wrong in your marriage. Can we discuss that for a minute."

"Primarily my work. Although I wasn't particularly successful, I put in a strong effort, way too many hours. Establishing a career was my first focus back then. Laura Anne was busy with the baby and her volunteer work at the hospital. We employed a reliable neighborhood girl to babysit so Laura Anne could come and go as she wished including lots of time out with friends. When I was home, I was tired and not interested in doing much."

I averted my eyes. Guys can be so dumb. How many women over the years had told me they craved more attention from their husband?

Zachary added, "Even though we didn't spend much time together, I didn't see the affair coming."

"From what you said, it hit you hard?" I glanced over at Jenny, still engrossed in her book.

"I signed the divorce papers with my chin on my chest. I was making enough to support us, but not much for frills. Laura Anne wanted lots more, and the Duke could provide it. I knew I'd failed her and us on every level. I'd never felt such shame before in my entire life." A sudden blush spread over his face.

Zachary had humbly communicated his devastation.

"I thought our love would last forever," he concluded.

"How painful, I'm so sorry. Sadly, many times I've witnessed women throwing away a man's love for material wealth, even sometimes worthless promises. Deep regret often follows."

Zachary's lower middle class past came out in bits and pieces between more interruptions from British Airways accommodating first class flight attendants offering snacks and magazines. Laura Anne was his first real girlfriend. He'd been shy in school and, despite being good-looking, suffered from poor self-esteem due to an over-bearing father.

"Describe Laura Anne," I said sipping my ginger ale.

"She was beautiful, very outgoing, probably still is."

He reached for his wallet and pulled out a folded photograph. "This is my last picture of us. I'm sure our daughter must be gorgeous. I haven't seen her for so long, I wouldn't know her."

"You have no photos?"

"Laura Anne refuses to send me pictures."

I shook my head. "There's no reason to torture you like that."

"Maybe I deserved it. When she wanted out of our marriage, I didn't handle the breakup well and sort of disappeared afterwards."

"A double loss of wife and daughter...how difficult."

He rubbed his hands together. "Now I see families around me all the time, in restaurants, at parks. I'd like for somebody to call me Dad and act like I'm important to their world. Is that selfish?"

"Zachary, it's perfectly natural. As long as you keep in mind that children don't exist simply for the purpose of giving you pleasure." I glanced over at Jenny as we spoke. She'd dozed off with her head on Nick's shoulder.

"I realize that. I'm not stupid."

"Good. A child's presence in your life is wonderful, but temporary. Your job is to equip each offspring to fulfill God's purpose for his or her life. After all, they are His children foremost."

"I think I can do that now."

"I believe you will." For emphasis, I punched my fist triumphantly in the sky, "You are very capable of being a great dad, Zachary!"

From the front of the plane, I heard the sound of silverware being shuffled about. "That's enough for now. Looks like our attendants are preparing to serve us."

Our meal was a choice of chicken Kiev or poached salmon in dill sauce. The flight attendants continued to tread the first-class aisles regularly with beverages, ice cream treats, nuts. Starvation or dehydration on British Airways is unlikely. So is rest with all the interruptions.

After we ate, I closed my eyes. The hum of the plane soothed me to sleep for several hours.

I awoke with the sunrise and opened my phone to read a few Psalms and pray silently for our day. We disembarked at Heathrow Airport at ten-thirty A.M., four-thirty P.M. Chicago time. Six hours of my life were gone forever, never having been lived on earth. Actually suspended somewhere in the air. A weird feeling.

At baggage claim two German shepherds on chains held by armed handlers walked the periphery of the luggage conveyor sniffing baggage.

I nudged Nick. "Scary looking reception. If I were a drug-carrier, my armpits would be soaked from fear. Those are serious-looking animals not to be messed with."

"Won't see this in Lake Geneva on your way to work," Nick commented.

I smiled. "Cross-continental travel is above all an exercise of attitude control due to exposure to the unfamiliar, which is why I love it."

After collecting our bags, we stood in a block-long queue (European for line I explained to Jenny) waiting our turn to enter one of London's cabs.

These were truly elegant taxis, not tired old cars like the ones that jam the streets of Chicago and Washington, D.C. Finally we were next in line. The courteous driver popped out and picked up our pieces of luggage like boxes of Kleenex.

A huge open section in the back of our taxi accommodated luggage. We had spacious seating with no room wasted by a trunk compartment.

"Where to, Sir?"

"The London Metropole on Edgeware Drive," Zachary announced from the front passenger seat. I sensed from the sound of his voice Zachary was a bit shaky off his home turf.

"Zachary," Nick asked conversationally, "Have you been to Europe before?"

"Never, I prefer good old American soil under my feet and have no intention of returning once we've completed our business."

I stopped my tongue before saying, Let's hope you won't have to.

CHAPTER FOUR

I followed our route as best I could on the map of London I'd printed out. No small feat.

"Every two blocks the street names change," I observed aloud. "Good thing I'm not behind the wheel." I'm still old-fashioned enough to like having a paper map in my hands at times, especially in unfamiliar locales in case my GPS doesn't work.

"According to my travel agent, our hotel, is only fifteen minutes from Heathrow, and centrally located."

I sat back to enjoy the sites of London.

At the Metropole the doorman assisted us in exiting the car with our baggage. Zachary had exchanged money at the airport and paid the cabdriver with what looked like Monopoly money. Our rooms were side by side on the fifteenth floor. We set a meeting time and separated.

I gasped when Nick opened the door. "This is awesome in every detail." I ran to the window. "Look at the amazing views of London." I plopped on the bed. "And thick white comforters which I love. The streets are pulsating with life and light. I can't wait to hit the sidewalks."

"Welcome to M/M Trevor" showed up on the TV screen in the sitting area with information on all sorts of hotel minutiae provided for our comfort. I checked the restaurant menu, noted the equipment in the exercise room, which included elliptical, always my first choice. In the bath, thick white towels hung over a U-shaped heating rod, warm to the touch. "Nick, I need a heater like this for home," I joked.

"Sure, we'll get three, put it on your Christmas wish list."

"Very funny." I yawned. I'd been warned by a friend not to go to sleep when we arrived.

"Just forty winks," Nick insisted. We all snuggled on the bed and passed out for thirty-five minutes.

So much for surviving jet lag and fitting in.

Zachary's travel agent had wisely planned half a day in London to adjust our body clocks before connecting with Laura Anne and Ashley. "You'll thank me," she guaranteed.

When we awoke, Nick, Jenny, and I took off to explore while Zachary handled his work e-mails.

Setting off by foot on our self-guided walking tour, we discovered a picnic bench on Bond Street where FDR and Churchill sat talking, frozen forever in bronze. The sculptor had kindly left space on the bench between them for a third person. I occupied it briefly pretending to give advice to the old chaps while Jenny took my picture.

At the next corner, Nick yelled, "Jennifer, watch out!" as he yanked my arm to rescue me from a car coming within inches of my legs.

"Sweetheart, don't you see the large capital letters painted at the street intersections that remind pedestrians to 'Look right, look left' before crossing? Remember, motorists drive on the opposite side of the road here."

Humbled I said, "Forgot, I was too absorbed in the historic sights all around me. Jenny, make sure you keep holding Daddy's hand!"

After my near fatality, we made it to Trafalgar Square to check out St. Paul's Cathedral and Westminster Abbey for their docent tours. We managed to get in on the tail end of one. "This is the location for coronations of forty British monarchs. 3000 famous Britons are buried beneath the magnificent building. It's been standing since well before the birth of America."

After the energetic guide finished, I said, "Nick, I find it hard to wrap my head around all this solemn splendor of Westminster Abbey. The stained glass of cathedrals leaves me in awe that God gives such creative abilities to men."

He agreed and pulled me and Jenny away to see a painting another tour guide was describing. "Sir Walter Raleigh was beheaded. Supposedly his wife kept his head in a velvet bag to show her visitors."

I whispered to Nick, "I remembered him laying down his coat to be walked over. How did he manage to fall so incredibly out of her favor? Behave yourself, husband."

Nick chuckled. "I'll try, wife."

Next, we scurried through the Marks and Spencer department store, selecting a few games and collector dolls for Ashley. The exchange rate wasn't great, but it wouldn't keep anyone from shopping. I was saddened by the sight of homeless people of all ages on the streets. Evidently this problem wasn't exclusive to our American cities.

We rushed through because the customary female gene for shopping passed me by. The quicker I'm in and out of a store, the better, plus we didn't want to miss the enthralling Changing of the Guards.

I nudged Nick. "History has a way of putting present day life in perspective."

Jenny pestered us to see Madame Tussaud's Wax Museum after seeing a poster enticement.

Nick looked at my map. "No, too far to go," but he took my picture next to the life-sized billboard picture of Agatha Christie seated in an armchair. He joked, "'Sister sleuths' is what I'm going to call this."

"We don't look anything alike. My hair, light brown with gold glints, is shoulder length. Agatha has short grey hair, but I'll take the mystery-solving comparison any day."

Nick squeezed my hand. “It’s true, you’ve an intuition about people, Jennifer. You already solved several mysteries Miss Marple style.”

“How kind of you , my dear husband.”

Nick, Jenny and I scurried about the National Gallery of Art, along with half the tourists in London, before hurrying to Buckingham Palace in time for the changing of the guard.

When we finally returned to the hotel, I was exhausted, but not my energetic Nick. “I’m heading to the weight room. Want to come?”

“Thanks, I’ve had enough exercise on London’s pavements.”

By six we’d freshened up and dragged ourselves to meet Zachary for dinner in the nineteenth-floor hotel restaurant overlooking this gorgeous city sparkling with lights.

Once we ordered, red snapper and blackened grouper for Nick and me, filet mignon for Zachary and mac and cheese for Jenny, I reintroduced the subject of Laura Anne. “How would you describe her personality?”

Zachary gazed at me with a vague expression. “Remember I haven’t seen her for years, and our communication never was sparkling.”

“Of course, I understand and I don’t want to speculate on what kind of woman Laura Anne will be now. From what I’ve heard about her, my imagination is conjuring up someone highly unpleasant. I hope I’m wrong.”

"Sadly I can say nothing to change your opinion." Zachary frowned. "I hope we're both mistaken for the sake of my daughter."

I collapsed in bed at ten o'clock. If I'd known what the next day would bring, I'd never have wanted to leave the city of London.

CHAPTER FIVE

Tuesday morning we ate a hearty English breakfast of eggs, grilled tomatoes and a meat named bacon which actually resembled what we call ham in the States.

"This is the day you meet the daughter you haven't seen for eight years." Nick put into words what we all were thinking.

Quickly we returned to our rooms, re-packed our bags and met in the lounge for our taxi van to drive us to the castle.

"Are you nervous?" Jenny asked Zachary with child-like naiveté.

Zachary clutched his chest. "Petrified!"

I liked his honest answer.

"Mr. Taylor, don't worry," Jenny reassured him. "I'm sure your daughter will like you. I already do."

I laughed. "Nothing like being encouraged by a child."

By nine we were off for a two-hour drive to Laura Anne and Duke George's castle home, Wycham Manor in western England. I reveled in the green and brown Cotswolds territory we passed through, like a fairyland with quaint cottages. The road, rainy, mist-laden added to the ambiance.

Zachary and I sat side by side maximizing use of our time to confer along the way. "Did Laura Anne tell you her plans for our evening at her home?"

"Castle, you mean. There's sixteen bedrooms on the third floor alone."

I tried not to look surprised at such opulence.

He continued, "Laura Anne messaged me that we'll have a formal dinner followed by musical entertainment with a few extended family members in attendance. She assured me in her words, 'I'll arrange everything for our trip starting the next day.' The woman likes to be in control and have things totally her way. Fine by me, I'm not going to stir any conflict over unimportant details."

"Very wise."

Zachary got a faraway look and became quiet and pensive. "You know how important this is to me, Jennifer?"

"Yes, Zachary, I do." I patted his arm. For his sake, I hoped this worked out. Concern washed over me. I prayed quietly, "May Zachary experience the great joy of fatherhood, Lord."

Zachary added emphatically, "I figure I can tolerate anything for a few days to gain custody of my daughter."

It was my turn to withdraw into thought. Was Zachary a ticket to a free flow of cash for Laura Anne? How much was he prepared to pay for this custody agreement? I imagined Laura Anne would have high expectations. I chose to let Nick work through those financial details with him and concentrate on the emotional aspects.

"Okay, Zachary, let's go over a few more pointers. Keep in mind that it's best if you don't show too much affection to Ashley immediately. A child Ashley's age will not want to be gushed over. A simple hug to start. Give her time. Be polite and interested, but not overpowering, okay?"

He clicked his tongue. "I'll try. I've never been this tense." He confessed, "When nervous I've been known to chatter. Who knows what I might say? Shut me up if I get carried away."

I squeezed his shoulder. "Don't worry. This will go fine."

"Sure it will." His tone of false bravado was unmistakable.

"The key, Zachary, is just be yourself." The second the words were out, I wanted to push them back into my mouth. That's not the thing to tell someone with a history of rejection and low self-esteem. Deeply hurt people often grow up insecure and don't appreciate who they are. At times, they even wish to be somebody else they admire. It's common for wounded people to constantly measure how different they are, instead of valuing their uniqueness.

"And how exactly do I do that? Obviously, it didn't work for me before in my relationship with Laura Anne."

"Zachary, let's focus on the facts in your life now. You learned to feel safe and competent in your business environment and have become highly successful. That's a huge accomplishment. You're not who you were."

He agreed. I sensed a slight lift in his shoulders.

Sadly, Laura Anne had placed him in this painful, insecure relational territory again.

When we pulled onto the castle drive, my mouth dropped open. Zachary hadn't exaggerated. The Duke and Laura Anne lived in a real castle, complete with turrets, acres of land, a large pond poking out behind the house.

Magnificent English gardens shot out from the building in multiple directions. The mammoth maze of hedges, interrupted at precise intervals by perfect squares was filled with lush roses and other flowering plants, accentuating the entrance. The summer had been unseasonably warm. Peach roses, the size of my hand, were only now beginning to lose their petals.

At the end of the drive, a thick, oak door swung open revealing an expressionless female maid in a perky black and white uniform. Upon drawing closer, I saw she wore an engraved name pin, Valerie. To my surprise, Valerie actually curtsied.

"Good afternoon, welcome to Wycham Manor." Valerie's cold tone was followed by a gracious hand gesture as she directed us into a reception foyer as high as it was wide—twenty feet at least. I tried not to gawk at the gorgeous ceiling with carved moldings and angels on rosettes that encircled three chandeliers each the width of a dining room table.

The interior walls appeared to be poured concrete with speckled texture softened by hanging tapestries the size of Persian carpets on the walls. A framed picture in a four-by-eight-foot gold frame of a woman in a ball gown was the focal point of the sitting room to our left. This was none other than Laura Anne, I assumed, mistress of the manor.

I checked the walls for other family pictures hoping to see Zachary's daughter Ashley. None. Perhaps Laura Anne displayed personal photos in her bedroom. Or had Laura Anne removed them thinking it would be too painful to see her daughter after Ashley went to live in the States. Strange there were no pictures of the Duke either although I noticed the outline of several frames on the wall where pictures apparently had previously been.

Laura Anne swished into the room in a teal blue afternoon gown. I recognized her instantly from the painting. Honey-colored hair, soft and thick, draped her shoulders. If it was bleached, not even a hint of dark root crept into view.

With a waist far smaller than her shoulders, and hips gently rounding her flat stomach, Laura Anne could easily be mistaken for a movie star. She carried herself with magnetic energy, like something was about to happen at any minute and it would be wonderful.

I suspected Laura Anne was the kind of girl everyone clustered around in high school, in contrast to me, too introspective to want to be part of such a group. However, I always knew how to speak my mind when needed.

Our attentive hostess, the Duchess of Wycham Manor, presented us with her smile. Simultaneously, I felt as if we were being scanned and entered onto an invisible computer screen of her brain. She gave each of us a cheek kiss. Pure social custom, I was sure, even extending a kiss to Zachary. Her eyes never lost their self-absorbed assessing.

Meanwhile, I was making my own evaluation. This woman liked to be in charge. No doubt there. Zachary was right. I handed Laura Anne my card before she asked for it. I knew she would, yet I was certain I'd already been thoroughly checked out.

Laura Anne held the card aloft and read aloud, Jennifer Trevor, Psychotherapist, Individual, Marriage, and Family Counseling. "How long have you been in practice, may I ask?"

I smiled again, sure she knew before I arrived on her doorstep. This brief interrogation was simply to show me my place in our relationship. "Over ten years, Laura Anne. May I call you that?"

"Of course. What a wonderful idea Zachary had to bring you." Laura Anne's words poured out like thick cream. "I'm so glad your husband and daughter could come along also. Dawson will settle your bags in your rooms. We'll have tea in the sitting room. Do you need to freshen up first?"

She made the words sound like I was a wilting flower in need of perking. Maybe I did, but I wasn't going to oblige her by leaving Zachary unattended just yet.

"I can wait," I said, sweetly I hoped.

"Where's Ashley?" Zachary asked impatiently.

Laura Anne's face took on a blank expression. "Darling, she's not here." Her sapphire eyes watched Zachary closely, pleased I was certain at his obvious disappointment. Laura Anne turned to the lowboy and began to fuss with tea things.

It took Zachary several seconds to find his voice. "What do you mean?" He sounded confused, and I heard fear, too. I understood why Laura Anne might not want me around. She played with his emotions like a cat plays with yarn.

"Don't worry, darling, she's at boarding school. You'll see her tomorrow. I thought it best we have this evening alone to work through our business arrangements."

I sighed loud enough for both of us. No warning for Zachary! How cruel. I already didn't like this woman.

"Couldn't you have thought to mention this little detail?" Zachary said sarcastically.

"Darling, you assumed she'd be here! I never said so. You always had a problem with assumptions."

Zachary noisily clicked his cup down on his saucer. "Like expecting honest communication and reasonable behavior."

His words surprised me, he was expressing his anger quite well. I had misjudged him as totally passive, but then there's no way to know for certain what the relationship between two people is without seeing it lived out before you. Still Zachary was very wise to have support present. He hadn't underestimated his callous assessment of his wife.

"May I see a picture of Ashley?" he asked. "You must have recent pictures about."

Laura Anne passed a plate of miniature tea cakes before she answered.

"Darling, you know I never was one for pictures. I'm not particularly fond of capturing people digitally or on film. I prefer my memories. The few I have I've packed away to prepare myself for being without my daughter. You can take your own pictures tomorrow."

Almost on cue, Nick and I looked at the picture of Laura Anne on the wall behind her head.

She followed our gaze. "George insisted on that portrait," she shrugged. "Now as to our business, I've planned a wonderful trip for us, but tonight my chef has prepared a delicious welcoming feast."

"I bet you have," Zachary muttered.

Laura Anne glanced at him and pouted. "You must give me a chance. I've made every effort to make this work for you, Zachary. We're going to Scotland to holiday and sight-see. It'll be very casual and informal, a different setting than Ashley's lovely home."

I marveled that she could suggest this cold citadel was a pleasant home but said nothing.

"Jennifer and her daughter will accompany us." Zachary spoke forcefully. "Her husband, Nick, who is my lawyer, leaves tomorrow on a short golfing holiday."

"Of course, as you wish," Laura Anne said petulantly. "We'll talk more about the arrangements after dinner."

Zachary's eyes were black, but he held up his hand as if to say, "Okay we're done for now."

I intended of course to be present for that discussion not just to protect Zachary's interests. I didn't trust this woman to keep her hands off my man, any man, although I had complete confidence in my husband. He has two passions, Jesus Christ and me, in that order. I used to come first, but second is fine now. Who can argue with Jesus first?

"It won't take long," Nick added. "I need your signature on the simple contract I faxed. I assume you read it?"

"Of course," Laura Anne purred. "I made a few changes we can discuss after dinner in the library.

I felt an ominous chill, but silently finished my tea.

"Dinner will be at seven. You'll meet my husband, Duke George at dinner. Perhaps you'd like a short nap. Now if you'll excuse me, I must finish packing for our trip. Valerie, my maid, will make you comfortable." Laura Anne yanked a bell pull, and the maid who had ushered us in appeared silently as a cat.

"Valerie, please show our guests to their rooms."

As we walked to the guest wing Zachary muttered, "Isn't our culture wonderful? At dinner I get to face the guy I wanted to kill eight years ago."

Valerie looked back sharply. I wished he hadn't used those words. They would come back and haunt us later.

CHAPTER SIX

The elegant bathroom in our suite was the size of my family room. After a brief rest, I showered, then slipped my cream-colored knit dress over my bra, half-slip and opaque hose. I rummaged through the velvet jewelry bag I'd brought for my pearl pendant with its tear-shaped black onyx stone.

Nick hung it around my neck and kissed my cheek, whispering, "I wish we had more time alone."

I smiled. "Me too."

"I'll be holding you to that later."

"Good." I grinned.

Nick straightened his tie. "I'll meet you downstairs after I go over some of the legal details for our meeting later."

"Okay, sweetie."

I stuck matching pearl earrings through my ear lobes and stepped back to check myself in the full-length mirror. Simple, yet elegant, exactly the look I wanted.

Jenny entered our room wearing the floral shirtwaist I'd laid on her bed. "This house, I mean castle, is amazing, Mom. I've been exploring."

"Stay close, honey, it's almost time for dinner."

Dawson the butler/chauffeur knocked on our doors to inform Zachary, Nick and me that the cocktail hour was beginning.

When I descended the spiral staircase, I had a momentary flashback to Scarlet O'Hara's scene from *Gone With the Wind* as she floated down to greet Rhett Butler which made me chuckle.

It was my intention to have fun on this trip. I take seriously the Scripture command, "This is the day the Lord has made, let us rejoice in it."

Still, after my first meeting with Laura Anne, I braced myself internally. I decided nothing she did would unsettle me. At least that's what I hoped.

At the moment, food became primary in my mind. I was famished and eager to imbibe an English dinner enjoyed by royalty, whatever that turned out to be.

Laura Anne met us in the reception foyer. Other guests, dressed formally for dinner, were already milling about. She cheerily made introductions. "My brother-in-law Richard, also our lawyer, is joining us with his wife, Constance. And come meet George's Aunt Rosalind."

Aunt Rosalind was almost six feet tall, with wide shoulders. Her face, oval with high cheek bones, gave her a distinguished look. Although her skin showed fine etchings of age around electric green eyes and across her brow, there was very little sagging around her cheeks or mouth. Her hair, an auburn, probably had help from liquid in a bottle to keep its vibrant color.

Jenny greeted her politely then said with typical nine-year-old bluntness, "You don't look like an aunt. You're not old enough."

Rosalind put her arm around Jenny and laughed with a hoarse, infectious sound as she beamed at Jenny. "I'm going to take that for a compliment. We're going to be great friends."

We made polite small talk while waiting for dinner to be announced.

Laura Anne strolled over and took my arm to lead me to the table. Despite her warm fingers, I felt she was as approachable as a knight in a metal suit.

Duke George made his entrance formally after we were all seated at the table. He stood behind his chair briefly, then took his place at the head with his aunt to his left and wife on the right.

I studied him carefully. His hair had started to recede leaving a two-inch-sized area of bald flesh. The duke was shorter than Zachary, I'd guess five-nine. From the looks of his belly, the Duke didn't exercise enough and ate quite well.

Evidently Laura Anne realized physical attraction was shallow. Yet, I couldn't help but wonder if this love affair was wallet-deep.

Duke George reached over and patted his wife's hand. Then his eyes immediately circled our gathering.

When the Duke spoke, his charm was evident. "One of the first things that attracted me to my lovely wife was her American accent which fascinated me. I'm delighted to have even more Americans at my table tonight."

Laura Anne flashed him a smile as a reward. She seemed to enjoy the compliment even if it was past tense. For all her facade of composure and sophistication, did a needy child's ego lurk inside her?

Duke George continued to dominate the conversation with stories about his visit to America.

The meal, a four-course affair of amazing fragrance and food, carrot-coriander soup, salad, succulent green beans, sirloin steak and turkey was scrumptious.

"I understand you're here because we're making new arrangements for our daughter's custody. Not having Ashley will create a void in our life," the Duke said as he rubbed Laura Anne's back lightly. "But we'll adjust somehow, right, darling?"

She flashed him an impassive look. "Yes, dear."

Duke George shifted to inquiries of us. "Are you walkers, Mr. & Ms. Trevor? We've marvelous trails here. Or perhaps you prefer other sports?"

"Doctor and Mr. Trevor," Laura Anne corrected him.

Duke George looked at Nick, studying him for the first time. "Who's the lawyer?"

"I am. My wife has the doctorate. To answer your question I enjoy golf and tennis."

Lifting his water glass, the Duke sipped from it before commenting. "Good choices. I golf every Thursday and Saturday morning with my sticks and often disobedient white balls at Scrag Hill Golf Course. I find it adds frustration and agony to otherwise gorgeous days. A shame you won't be here long enough to join me."

"I have a golf excursion to Scotland planned, otherwise I certainly would enjoy it."

"George, you're the first duke we've met," I said. "Other than golf, how does a duke typically spend his days?"

Duke George laboriously described his family background and his investment work with nonchalant and disparaging comments, only interrupting himself to scold the maid when she tried to remove his plate before he'd finished.

Everyone in his family must be accustomed to his soliloquies I concluded because no one made an effort to interrupt George.

Nick smiled at George's dry English humor. I found him rather arrogant and self-centered but overall likable. He reminded me of a grouchy grandpa who taunted others for the joy of it.

I half-listened to him as I studied the other guests.

My full attention returned to Duke George when he said, "Rosalind, I need to warn my guests that you're a brilliant woman except for one major inconsistency." He looked first at Nick, then me. The Duke seemed to purposely ignore Zachary altogether. "Aunt Rosalind's a capable stockbroker who can outplay anyone I know in the market. But she's one of those rare birds, a Christian. She'll talk your head off about it if you let her."

Rosalind adjusted her rope of pearls.

Acting the gracious hostess, Laura Anne intervened. "George, how nastily you put it. Darling, that's enough teasing. We need to talk about tomorrow's trip."

Duke George's eyes sparkled. "Humor me, darling, this is the only time I have with you and your guests." He directed his next remarks at us. "My aunt keeps telling me I need God's help to be transformed, because you can't change yourself. I ask her why would I want to? I like myself as I am."

Nick caught Rosalind's eye and winked. "As a matter of fact, I'm a Christian and I needed lots of changing."

Duke George groaned. "Not two! Maybe three?" George stared at me. "How about you, dear? Where do you stand on the theory?"

My skin prickled. I greatly dislike being called "dear." And the word theory for my Christian beliefs was frankly offensive.

Nick nudged my knee then winced, apparently anticipating my reply.

Rosalind answered first. "Theory, my nephew? It's more than that." Rosalind looked at me with new interest. "What keeps anyone from believing the truth?"

Duke George jumped in before I could answer. "A major turnoff for me is the fact that there are so many different denominations all professing to have the truth. Then they verbally stab one another every chance they get."

"I agree that can be sad," Rosalind agreed, "but there's more agreement among genuine Christian churches than disagreement. The Christian faith is like the trunk of a huge tree. Denominations are various branches."

Zachary set down his fork. "There's a common basis. Genuine Christians all believe in one God as three persons, Father, Son and Spirit. Also that Jesus was born of a virgin, suffered, died, and rose. His action created freedom from sin for anyone who believes in Him."

This was not typical dinner conversation, but I wasn't opposed to going with the flow.

Duke George bristled. "Actually I have trouble with your concept of sin. Quite honestly, I don't feel like a sinner. I question the need to depend on a savior. And I don't require a distant God to help me do what I can handle myself."

"He is not distant when you truly know him." Rosalind turned to look pointedly at Duke George. "As for the self-sufficiency argument, you are important to God. But you may not be ready to depend upon Him, until you realize you can't do life as well on your own. You haven't come to that conclusion obviously."

Richard and his wife Constance looked uncomfortable. Heads down, they busily devoured their meal.

"Rosalind, it's sweet of you to care about me," Duke George said. "It really is, aunt."

Overall, the Duke seemed to enjoy the conversation. He added, "Wasn't that a nice lead-in I gave you, Aunt Rosalind?" George's voice was rich with sarcasm and thick with too much wine. He apparently had started earlier, because I only saw him drink one glass during dinner. "Why don't you tell them about our English wars between the Anglicans and the Catholics and our saints."

Her good humor became short-lived. "I won't stand for bashing the Christian religion in my presence. God cares for everyone who puts their faith in Him." Rosalind set her water glass down loudly.

I intervened. "Rosalind, I also believe in a caring, personal God who answers our prayers. When I ask for help in a situation, I go straight to the top, just like I would in a business."

"Perhaps we can have this discussion another time," Laura Anne said.

Duke George added, "All this banter aside, I admire Aunt Rosalind greatly for the good that she does through her various church organizations. She's the closest thing to a saint I've seen."

Laura Anne pouted. "Darling, what about me!"

"Of course, my sweet. Your sainthood is indisputable."

His tone was sarcastic. Evidently Laura Anne picked up on that because she glared at him.

"Duke George, you talk as if you've been giving God some thought," Nick commented.

Duke George stabbed his finger at his chest as if in shock. "Me! Never! Fascinating subject religion, but one of the no-no's socially. It appalls Laura Anne when I bring it up."

"Which you do often." Laura Anne smiled grimly at him and twisted her dessert fork.

Something was obviously strained in their relationship.

We finished our meal discussing England's weather and the various hiking paths throughout the area. The dessert was chocolate cheesecake dripping with fudge sauce and a dessert liqueur. The chef cooked expertly, no doubt about it.

After the food was cleared, Nick leaned forward on the table. "Laura Anne, forgive me for interrupting this pleasant social time with business. As you know I'm representing Mr. Taylor. We need to work out several details before I leave tomorrow to connect with my golf group."

"Of course, we'll do that now." She gave Nick a coy smile.

We paraded toward the library to settle Ashley and Zachary's future I hoped. On the way, I managed to pull Nick aside briefly to whisper privately, "I might have known Laura Anne wouldn't meet without her lawyer."

My easy-going husband shrugged in a "so-what" gesture. "No problem. That's actually good to expedite things. Don't worry, we'll make it work."

The library could easily hold fifty people. I looked around at the paneling, rich, dark oak, brightened by framed portraits of kings and queens. Maybe they were only princes and princesses. How would I know? Massive carved chairs lined one wall. I'd sit in them only if exhausted. They suggested all the comfort of a torture rack. Long tapestry-like drapes covered the tall windows behind the desk.

Zachary seated himself next to me and mumbled in my ear. "Great. A group." I knew he considered me his source of security and liked me to stay close. I hoped I could provide as much comfort as Jenny's Winnie the Pooh quilt did for her.

Revolvers, mostly antique, were shaped in a perfect circle as a wall decoration with their handles extending like rays. Another wall displayed several large, heavy swords. Not my favorite decor. I desperately hoped Laura Anne didn't have misery waiting for Zachary in this somber chamber.

Duke George walked over and put his arm on the back of Laura Anne's chair. "As you know, my dear, I refuse to let business intrude overly into our lifestyle and never into my after-dinner drinks. You'll excuse me."

She avoided looking at him as he exited the room.

Nick spoke first. "We have some personal matters to discuss, Laura Anne. Do you wish to include all your guests?" How could he tactfully say get Rosalind and Constance out of here please? Dawson, the butler/chauffeur serving after-dinner aperitifs should be dismissed also. Richard, her lawyer brother-in-law, could remain.

Laura Anne's reply was swift. "Of course everyone can be here. They can hear about anything that concerns me."

I glanced at Zachary. Didn't it occur to Laura Anne that the issue involved Zachary, and he might not share her feelings? Was he okay with this?

Before I could open my mouth to comment, Zachary said, "Have it your way." His hands were a study in control.

If only he knew how to fight back when they lived together, I wondered if their marriage might have held together. I took another look at the ice cube eyes of Laura Anne and got my answer. Not a chance.

Being in this unnatural social/business situation was unsettling. Searching for conversation has never been my problem. Typically words flow. Nothing was natural about this. Fortunately it wasn't my place to say much.

Laura Anne, I'd guess to no one's surprise, took charge. "Now to start. I know you were expecting Ashley to be here, that's regrettable. Obviously, she's not, but the nanny will collect her from boarding school and bring her to meet us in Scotland tomorrow. Then we'll visit Edinburgh and Perth, charming towns you'll love."

"How lovely," Zachary said mocking Laura Anne's favorite word.

Nick said, "Alright, let's move on. We can arrange to get Ashley's school and medical records transferred, Laura Anne, unless you prefer to handle that."

Richard, Laura Anne's lawyer-brother-in-law, approached her and whispered his advisements.

Nick continued. "Most importantly, I want to know if we're in agreement on the terms I faxed."

Instead of answering Nick, Laura Anne presented another document to Zachary. Evidently, she had drawn up more stipulations she wanted him to accept. This led to a lengthy discussion among them.

In conclusion, Zachary agreed to approving her plan almost in entirety, changing only minor details.

Laura Anne flashed a smile at Zachary. "See how well this is going! But you know I can't possibly sign a thing tonight, until I'm sure Ashley and Zachary get on well." She waved her hand in the air.

Nick, Zachary and Richard, conferred again.

Time for me to intervene I decided. I said, "Laura Anne, you do realize their father-daughter relationship will need more time to develop? A few days is hardly sufficient for any type of evaluation."

"I understand, I just want to make sure there's no initial adjustment problem..."

Zachary interrupted her. "I'd hoped to persuade you to forego..."

"My mind is made up about this trial period. I have no intention of changing it. After all this is my baby I'm giving up." Laura Anne pulled out a handkerchief and delicately dabbed at her eyes. She spoke through trembling lips.

Laura Anne's apparent sadness at surrender of custody didn't make total sense since I knew Ashley had been away at school most of the time anyway. I tactfully put the fact out there. "Ashley's been living year around in a boarding school, correct?" I bit my lip to prevent saying, poor child.

"This has been terribly difficult. If it were up to me, I'd never surrender her. Life has gotten harder and harder. The Duke, well it's just not easy for him to be around children. Plus he's gotten more difficult as she aged. Ashley has tantrums over the silliest things. She's with me for every holiday though."

I felt a moment of compassion for Laura Anne before I plunged forward. "Then it's extremely wise that Ashley lives with her dad. He can give her an on-site parent plus psychological nurturing and professional counseling she may need at this critical age. It's a great plan!"

Nick jumped in, "Zachary has waited a long time, all the paperwork is in place. Could we just proceed?"

Laura Anne directed her answer to Zachary. "Yes, of course, but as I said I won't sign, not yet, I must be sure." Laura Anne stomped her silver slipper clad foot for emphasis.

I nodded and slipped a restraining hand on Nick's arm before he could say more.

Zachary sighed softly. "Alright, Laura Anne, we'll sign, after we return from this trip. I can wait a few more days."

I shivered. This arrangement sounded way too risky.

CHAPTER SEVEN

The rings beneath Zachary's eyes and his pallor the next morning made me wonder if he'd slept at all. I greeted him with "This is the day you see your daughter again, Zachary!"

"Finally!" He shot back.

We breakfasted quickly.

During the fifteen-minute wait for our limo's arrival, I suggested a brief walk. I wanted to speak to Zachary without risk of Laura Anne hearing.

Jenny stayed behind in the foyer, reading. Nick had been picked up at the first hint of dawn for his golfing excursion. I was thrilled for him. This trip would be golf heaven for my husband.

Zachary and I headed for the lion's head statuary outside the castle's front entrance. From there we took a brief walk through the English garden on our right.

When we were far enough out, I halted. "Be honest, Zachary, how are you?"

"Between my nerves, and the jet lag time change which is hitting me harder the second day, frankly I'm not in great shape."

I patted his arm, "You'll be better after you see Ashley in Edinburgh."

He grunted and swigged coffee from the paper cup he carried. Possibly his security tonic?

I spoke additional words of encouragement and then asked him if I could pray.

"Absolutely."

"Lord, we entrust this entire situation into your hands. May Zachary and Ashley have an awesome initial experience today, and may it be the start of a wonderful daddy-daughter relationship that lasts a lifetime."

My brief prayer perked him up visibly.

I was pleased that I'd accepted Zachary's invitation to assist with this bizarre situation. The dear man certainly needed help.

Back at the castle, Laura Anne was ready. To her credit she was prompt. We all climbed into the limo driven by Dawson and began our journey to the Brit Rail station.

Enroute, I reflected that Zachary, Laura Anne, Jenny and I were a strange group on a mission. I only hoped we were in one accord.

I opened my travel book to read about our destination, the city of Edinburgh, also called Auld Reekie from the days it was black with the smoke from coal and woodfires. The thought of a city centuries old seemed incomprehensible to my American mind.

We boarded the train without fanfare. I enjoyed speeding along on silvery rails, like a surrealistic experience. Europeans do train travel so efficiently.

The journey would be pleasant I'd decided in advance, committing myself to making the most of every moment. We had a small table between comfortable bench seats. Our car was next to the designated food car. From it passengers brought brown bags back to their seats. The smell of micro-waved breakfast platters with bacon and sausage wafted past us. Sit-down dining was also available, quite expensive, I concluded from a glance at the menu.

Along with my professional role of helping Zachary, I marveled at this amazing semi-vacation experience God had provided. The Lakes area of England had prepared me somewhat for the wild, rugged landscape at Scotland's border.

Laura Anne had her nose in a novel most of the time. Eventually it lulled her to sleep. Jenny had fallen asleep also, soon after we embarked.

I used the occasion to further coach Zachary There was so much to cover in our limited time.

He asked me about the best way to discipline Ashley saying, "I want to do this right."

"Of course. Think of discipline as teaching. If you love her well, and I know you will, she'll want to please you and respond to your rules. Actually, discipline is training more than correcting. When you teach Ashley proper behavior, it becomes her natural way of acting. Having been in a boarding school much of her life, we don't know how she'll respond to your guidelines – hopefully with submission, but perhaps rebellion at first from her prior situation. Whatever, it's important to establish your authority early with kindness, love and firmness."

"And exactly how do I do that?"

"First, examine anything good about the methods learned from your childhood and determine to eliminate what wasn't positive. Few of us had perfect parents. Unless you think this through, you'll most likely end up parenting as you were parented."

Zachary screwed up his face. "Frankly, I got in a lot of trouble as a kid. My parents pretty much ignored me and let me do whatever I wanted. When I became a teen, they gave me total independence."

I checked myself from saying, What a shame. That's why we have problem kids in this world. Instead I said, "Ignoring a child is never wise. I know you want to do right by Ashley. My e-book *Soaring As A Parent* can help you. I'll see that you get a copy." I smiled. "For sure, you don't want to contribute a spoiled, disrespectful child to society. You'll have to be very watchful. From prior work with affluent clients, I know they often refuse to risk children's displeasure by insisting on appropriate, courteous behavior. Instead they indulge in excessive indulgence."

"That won't be me."

"Good, because at times you'll have to say 'No' to something Ashley dearly wants, which isn't in her best interests. This may infuriate her. You have to be willing to tolerate temper tantrums, perhaps embarrassing behavior, even in public. Stick to your rules. Don't allow her to manipulate you, and you'll do fine."

To his credit, Zachary listened intently, and even made notes on his phone.

"One more thing, at times you'll need to allow adverse logical consequences to follow any poor choices Ashley may make. Yes, even if they frustrate her. That's how she'll learn."

"Okay, I get it. But I'll be calling you if I get stuck."

"Fine. I believe you'll do great. Of course, we can follow up in the States."

Zachary grinned. "Now, if you don't mind, I could use a ten-minute nap."

As the train glided into Waverley Station in Edinburgh, I stared mesmerized at this European city of contrasts. Treeless mountains served as backdrop for Edinburgh Castle which dominated the center of the town. I heard the faint sounds of animals' bellowing. Such a strange sensation to hear jungle sounds in the heart of a sophisticated, historic city.

Laura Anne stirred and lifted her head. "Wonderful, we've arrived just in time for our late lunch with Ashley. You'll love the cozy, quaint place where we're staying."

Much as I would enjoy seeing Scotland, I'd never have agreed to this trek to Edinburgh had I been consulted initially. Obviously, Ashley's unpredictable mother made the plans with total disregard for the comfort of her ex-husband who had just crossed the Atlantic. This didn't elevate my trust level regarding her or my respect.

Laura Anne had chosen a hotel near the National Zoo on Corstorphine Road. My cramped legs adjusted quickly to moving again on the busy sidewalk.

Inside, at the hotel reception area, Laura Anne handled check-in personally and confirmed our tour plans with the concierge.

After we'd settled into our rooms, we met again in the main area, a dark space, with olive-green walls and heavy, carved tables and chairs. Cascading velvet drapes seemed like shadows of weary giants guarding the windows.

The oppressive theme was carried into the restaurant's private reception room. Definitely not a cozy kid's environment.

Laura Anne planted herself on a chair in the middle of the room and flipped through a magazine she'd grabbed from the coffee table. "Ashley should be here any minute. Her nanny picked her up at her school and is bringing her directly."

Zachary perched on the edge of the sofa and alternated between sitting and standing.

Jenny approached him and blurted out, "I can't wait to meet your daughter."

"Me, too," he said.

My precious daughter Jenny is always open to new friends and adventures which makes her a good traveler. Fortunately she's as adaptable as an angel. Of course her iPhone helped fill her down time with games. Normally I'd restrict usage more, but on this trip, I only insisted on equal time reading books.

"No worries, I'll sit here with you, Zachary," I said.

He bent toward me, "Great! I don't know if I'm more nervous or thrilled. How do I look?"

"Like an excited dad." Otherwise less than wonderful, I refrained from saying. I wouldn't lie. His face was grey and his stomach was making weird noises. If Ashley didn't show up soon, I might be finding him some Pepto Bismol.

"Don't worry, children want to love their parents."

The door opened and nine-year old Ashley stood blinking in the dim light. Zachary was transfixed as a dad would be seeing his newborn baby in a hospital nursery. Years of separation were about to melt away I prayed.

Ashley, a pretty blonde girl with a round face, tip-toed forward. No mistaking Laura Anne's blondeness. Her hair was short with a fence of bangs across her fore-head that reached her eyebrows. A long blue jumper, the English word for sweater, topped her denim skirt above black Mary Jane shoes with one-inch heels.

Ashley stopped in her tracks when she drew closer. Her nanny nudged her, and she walked tentatively forward. No running to Laura Anne. Ashley said a stiff "Hello, mum," but her focus was on Zachary.

Zachary raised his right hand to his eyes, brushing away the sudden wetness. I could see strained veins popping out around his temples. He immediately approached and wrapped his arms around Ashley squeezing her gently. She looked surprised but timidly laid two stiff arms on Zachary's shoulders. He scooped her closer. Her face turned pale.

Everything around us seemed to be moving in slow motion as I watched.

Ashley's formal, "How do you do," was muffled against Zachary's chest.

I'd have preferred Zachary wait until Ashley was ready to initiate physical connection on her own, but so be it.

Zachary suddenly became chatty. "It's been a long time since I've seen my little girl." He repeated several times how happy he was.

Up close I saw that Ashley had brown eyes like Zachary and his chiseled facial features.

Meanwhile, Laura Anne grilled the nanny, then dismissed her.

Ashley's face became bright and eager when she answered Zachary's questions about school. Until then, her eyes were veiled, like she'd seen things best unseen and she was guarding them now. Perhaps problems with her family life, I guessed but couldn't be sure.

While Zachary made small talk with Ashley, Laura Anne shifted restlessly in her chair.

I tried to distract her with questions about Edinburgh. She answered curtly.

Ten minutes passed like this, but it seemed an hour. Finally, Laura Anne spoke directly to her daughter. "Ashley, as I told you, I've arranged this holiday with your dad since it's so long since you've seen him. After all this time, I thought it'd be good to have a few fun days together to reconnect. We're starting with a city open air bus tour." Laura Anne stressed the word "all" in Ashley's not seeing her dad for ages inferring perhaps that Zachary had deliberately stayed away during this time.

Ashley's smile shivered on tremulous lips, like a scared little waif. When he wasn't looking at her, Ashley stared at this man who'd come to reclaim her as his flesh and blood.

I wanted to scoop her up and hug her myself. Some kids just never get enough love, and she looked needy. Who wouldn't be, cooped up in a boarding school most of her life?

Jenny bounced in from the bathroom and immediately hooked onto Ashley. "I've been waiting to meet you. We're going to have such fun!"

Ashley smiled for the first time and finally began to breathe naturally. Like most kids, she seemed far more comfortable with children than adults.

Zachary's daughter is so worth this effort. I reminded myself so is every kid.

Briefly, I tried to imagine giving up Jenny. I view mothering as a privilege. What kind of mother would consent to give up her child unless it was for the child's good? Surrendering a child for adoption rather than having an abortion or allowing custody change for the benefit of a child takes an emotionally mature, selfless adult. I greatly admire these women.

I'd counseled several post-abortive women through the guilt following abortion which sometimes occurs years later. On the other hand, those who chose adoption know immediately they made a better choice. And their bodies are healthier for having completed a pregnancy, a fact not mentioned on the news – less risk of cancer, depression, or heart disease. God's natural way is always better.

Self-giving is not how I read Laura Anne. The characters in this scenario before me somehow didn't seem authentic. And strangely, I was a player as well.

"Ready to go?" Laura Anne rose from her chair.

Zachary glared, "Laura Anne, you've had eight years, give me a half hour with Ashley, then we'll start out."

I refrained from speaking and pretended to examine a tour map.

Zachary and the girls were happily chatting.

"Let's get some sunshine Laura Anne and wait outside." We exited through the thickly carpeted lobby. I slipped my arm through Laura Anne's in an attempt to distract her while we waited for our double-decker tour bus.

Several minutes later, Zachary, Ashley and Jenny met us outside at the designated pick-up location.

Once we'd boarded the bus, the tour guide began to rattle off interesting but non-memorable facts. "Edinburgh was chosen as capital over the city of Perth because of its natural fortifications."

We all chose to sit on the upper level for the best views. Ashley and Jenny sat side by side with Zachary in the seat behind them. Laura Anne and I occupied the seats directly across from them.

"I'm still recovering from jet lag," Jenny said loudly. "I'm a little tired."

Ashley grimaced. "What's jet lag?"

"Suddenly your body needs to make day turn into night, so you stay awake through the hours you're used to sleeping. It takes a bit of getting used to, but only lasts a few days." Jenny was a born teacher.

Zachary put his arm protectively on Ashley's shoulder. He added, "You'll experience that firsthand when you come back to America with me. It doesn't last long. You'll hardly notice."

Ashley smiled timidly up at him.

"Have you ever been to the United States?" Jenny asked Ashley.

She got a faraway look on her face. "Mom said I used to live there, but I don't remember anything. I want very much to go back."

"Here's our shopping stop," Laura Anne announced airily.

We stepped down briskly onto the crowded street.

Zachary laughed. "You know from our day in London, Jennifer, that I normally hate to shop, but today I'll make an exception." He took the hand of each of the girls and pressed them into his own. "Ready, set, let's go!"

"Mr. Taylor, you're being silly, but I like it." Jenny grinned.

We toured the Royal Mile and Princes Street, braving the nonstop human shopping stampede packing the pavements, the United Kingdom word for sidewalk.

Jenny gazed into store windows wide-eyed. "I wonder how much money gets spent here every day."

"Guess?" Zachary asked.

Jenny piped up with "A million dollars."

"That seems too high. What's the amount really?" Ashley wanted an accurate answer, which I liked. Her eagerness for precise knowledge would help her adjust to life in America. She had so much to learn.

I remembered I could use a new pair of black heels, but those in the shop windows had heels resembling kids' building blocks. Inside the store a clerk brought me a pair to try on like ones the Wicked Witch from Oz might wear. I sent them back. What depraved designer's mind pulled off the hoax that heavy, square heels were stylish?

We stopped in the Cancer Research Foundation charity store and the resale Scottish Council for Spastics founded in 1946. Laura Anne refused to enter with Zachary, the girls and me. Apparently shopping second-hand was beneath her.

I found two matching wool blazers for the girls in a maroon thick wool which looked adorable on them. I love a bargain and know immediately what I like.

While the girls were in the dressing room, I said to Zachary, "You'll want to teach Ashley to be generous and thrifty so she doesn't squander money foolishly."

When I handed Ashley her package, she thanked me, a good sign that she hadn't been too spoiled, although it was undoubtedly her first second-hand anything. I smiled with satisfaction.

As we wandered past local shops, I was pleased to observe Ashley was careful crossing streets. At the next corner, several homeless, middle-age boys were ganged together, begging like a pack of dogs. The tallest one started to speak, but Laura Anne hurried us past.

"May I skip lunch and give money to those boys instead?" Ashley begged. "Please, Mum."

Laura Anne looked annoyed, but fished in her purse for a pound. I gave a five-dollar bill to Jenny who ran back and dropped the money in the boys' large plastic cup.

What a generous, kind child Ashley is, I thought. I couldn't know if her temperament was due to Laura Anne's influence or her boarding school, but regardless I was delighted. Again, it would make her adjustment to life with Zachary in America easier.

Laura Anne led the way everywhere. We followed her like a Pied Piper. Zachary and I had silently agreed to accept her agenda. Neither of us wanted to upset any aspect of this intricate plan to get Ashley home with her real dad.

Truthfully, I was enjoying our excursion too. What's not to like about touring a grand European city?

We ducked into a quaint bookstore/bakery featuring artful, doughy creations. The pastries were irresistible - apple pies with sultana raisins and custard cakes.

I tried several times without success to occupy Laura Anne in chit-chat so Ashley and Zachary could bond, but Laura Anne usually butted into these conversations.

Still it could have been worse. I reminded myself in a few days this would be all over. How wrong I was.

CHAPTER EIGHT

We returned to our hotel around 5 P.M. Laura Anne disappeared to her room to rest until dinner. Zachary, Ashley, Jenny and I were in my suite's sitting area. The girls were playing the Connect-Four checker game we'd bought in London.

Zachary pulled me aside. "How do you think first day went?"

I reassured him from the comfy sofa where I was nestled. "I'm rejoicing. So far all seems to be going well. Let's give Ashley some time to relax with Jenny now. You go ahead and make your business calls. I'll hold the fort with the girls for an hour."

My plan was to spend time with Ashley to get to know her better and collect any data that could help Zachary with her transition.

The girls finished their game. Ashley perched on the grey leather side chair next to me and opened a Tommy

Smurlee and Grella Weller adventure book. I asked about her reading preferences, then moved on to her favorite foods and school subjects. She rattled off answers like a kid who has been around adults a lot and doesn't mind answering boring questions.

She was in the middle of telling me about her friends when Laura Anne popped through the door. "Couldn't fall asleep, decided to join you."

Sadly, that ended my personal conversation with Ashley. She seemed to clam up when her mother was present.

Laura Anne started chatting about the history of the sites we'd seen. Her conversation was mostly about her impressions. She didn't try to pull the girls into the conversation. Where did this woman get her self-centeredness?

Mother of the year, no way! I wasn't buying that. I sensed a huge discrepancy in her behavior. Laura Anne had another agenda I couldn't quite figure out.

Dinner was uneventful. Jenny and Ashley sat at the end of the table with Zachary and took turns telling riddles.

Our sleeping arrangements, which I'd insisted upon, were Ashley and Jenny sharing a room. It adjoined Laura Anne's at her request. Ashley, at least, wouldn't have to put up with her mother's hovering all night.

Laura Anne and I said goodnight to the girls. I returned to their room around ten to check on Jenny. She was asleep, but Ashley lay in her bed in the huge room with her eyes wide open. I hoped fear wasn't building inside her. It's an emotion that can't always be viewed externally or measured easily.

I settled down near her feet on the fleur-de-lis bedspread. "Ashley," I whispered, "I'm going to ask you something point-blank, okay? You don't have to answer if you don't want."

Ashley dragged herself up against her pillow.

"How do you feel about going to live with your dad in America?"

"Okay, I think, but really it's hard to imagine what it'll be like."

"Just to reassure you. Your dad is a very kind man. He'll make every effort to see to it that you're happy."

As if on cue, Laura Anne flounced in from her adjoining room. "Ashley needs her rest, Jennifer." She leaned over and hugged Ashley, "Goodnight my little princess." Was it my imagination or did Ashley turn away?

She directed her next words at me. "Conversation can wait until tomorrow when my daughter is more alert."

In effect, she was shooing me away. I didn't appreciate it but forced myself to be polite. "Sure. Just saying good night." I bent over and kissed Ashley and my sleeping Jenny on the forehead. "Sweet dreams, girls," I said softly and turned to go.

How considerate Laura Anne sounded. Strangely she didn't display behavior of a protective mother type by shipping her daughter off to school all year.

She was involved in every moment with her daughter now, probably interfering because Zachary was present.

Laura Anne said gruffly, “Get some sleep, Ashley. I’m turning off the light.”

“Mum, you know I don’t like the dark.”

Laura Anne pointedly held the door open for me.

“You’ll be fine.” Laura Anne snapped the light off.

Back in our room, I prayed. “Jesus, I’m having a problem throwing myself into preparing Zachary for fatherhood when deep down I question if it’s going to happen. Laura Anne’s behavior confuses me. Then again, why wouldn’t she proceed? I mean Laura Anne set this whole event up with us and her family. It would be hard to back out now and save face.”

I paused and sighed. “Lord, I have this impression that Laura Anne doesn’t seem to have been the kind of child who ever gave away one of her toys, even if she no longer wanted it. As an adult she’s probably no different.” I considered asking her outright if she actually intended to go through with this.

I walked down the hall and encountered Zachary leaving his room.

“Sorry to bother you. Can we talk a second?”

“Sure, let’s go into the lounge.”

Zachary slumped into the nearest chair. "I'm worried. Laura Anne's acting coyly sweet but excessively possessive. She gave me diet plans for all Ashley's meals. She's sending her off with a small wardrobe of clothes. What do you think?"

My thoughts exactly. Of course, this wasn't the first time we had discussed concerns.

"It's tough, Zachary. The plan is for Laura Anne to let Ashley go. We can only go by her words. To be forthright, I have no idea where this is heading. I pray that she follows through."

Zachary slowly dragged himself to his feet. He looked about to cry, as if someone had turned off his confidence switch.

"Poor Ashley," he said. "She's so sweet. If Laura Anne's setting me up, it would be the delicate sort of torture she delights in. But I can't imagine why she'd want to hurt our daughter with false expectations."

I bit my tongue. That's exactly what I feared could happen. "Hard to say. She acts rather indifferent toward Duke George, but who knows what goes on beyond their bedroom door."

"Did you ever know a woman who takes such pleasure being in total control of others? What kind of creature is she?" He looked at me. "There must be some psychological label for it. Laura Anne can be emotionally frigid when it suits her." Zachary words shot out with venom.

I couldn't let Zachary stay hopeless. New daddy jitters were stressing him too. "Nothing has changed. Remember this was all Laura Anne's idea. Of course it's a risk. We're doing all we can. God's in charge of the outcome. And he loves both you and Ashley unconditionally."

"You're right. I just needed to talk. Sorry, for keeping you up."

"No problem. I'd be concerned too in your place. Before you go, Zachary, how about if I pray with you?"

Zachary looked at me sheepishly. "Will it do any good?"

"Of course it will. Prayer is the most powerful force on earth."

He bowed his head, as did I. "God, we believe you've got this, and we pray the outcome will be great for Ashley and Zachary. Let's close with the Our Father, Jesus' favorite prayer."

After speaking the final words with fervor, "For thine is the kingdom, the power and the glory. Amen," I said. "Now it's time for a peaceful night's sleep."

CHAPTER NINE

Concern regarding Zachary's anxiety kept me awake several hours tossing and praying further. I like everything out in the open. I decided to be bold and approach Laura Anne the next morning before breakfast.

I messaged her to meet me. She charged into my room, her long night gown visible below her ivory satin robe. Poor thing. I observed her wary, sheepish look as if she knew this might be unpleasant.

"Thanks for coming. I need to ask you a personal question. Is there more to the story here, Laura Anne?"

"Whatever do you mean?" She lifted her chin.

"About giving up your daughter. I mean is this for real?"

"Whatever do you mean? You know what I told Zachary."

I placed both my hands on my hips. "I know what you said, but for some reason I'm having trouble believing you will. Why end the relationship you have with your only daughter by surrendering full custody?"

"It's only fair."

"Why now? Your answer doesn't seem to make sense. I'm only asking out of concern for Zachary. Is there something going on that you aren't disclosing?"

"Like what?" I could almost hear Laura Anne grinding her teeth.

"Is Ashley ill? Are you getting ready to divorce George? Maybe you don't want to bring Ashley into a new relationship because your new beau doesn't want kids and you can't leave Ashley behind with Duke George. Zachary is a better out. Is that it? Forgive me for being so blunt. I know I'm out of bounds here."

"Obviously, Jennifer, you don't think much of me. Have you ever considered that Ashley will benefit from her life in America? I did. Of course, I'll insist that she return to Oxford for college. I don't intend to lose her forever."

"Okay. That sounds reasonable." I sighed. "I want to believe you. I just need to be sure Zachary and Ashley don't get hurt. "

"Think positive, isn't that what counselors usually suggest?" She smiled at me slyly.

The rest of the day Laura Anne was definitely colder toward me. Not that I could blame her. Honestly, I didn't care. We motored to Perth where she'd booked rooms in a gorgeous, large Victorian B & B. We had a pleasant day touring the small shops in and around Perth.

Mid-afternoon we attended a quaint tea at the Sweet Lady Cafe with delicious blackberry scones and clotted cream. Then we headed back to rest at our bed and breakfast.

That afternoon at 5 P.M. Zachary pounded on my door. I lifted my face from Fodor's travel book on Scotland. His face was white.

"Ashley's missing. Jenny said she left the room to buy a candy bar in the B & B gift shop. Jenny fell asleep. That was nearly two hours ago. Ashley still hasn't returned." Zachary ran his palm across his forehead and flung it down. He looked frantic.

I touched his shoulder gently. "Try to be calm, Zachary. I'll help you look." We met Laura Anne in the lobby and together searched the bed and breakfast's public areas.

An hour later Laura Anne and Zachary were in my room listening as he dialed the authorities. The door was standing open. I saw Ashley get off the elevator and head for her room. I rushed to the door. "Ashley!"

Laura Anne shouted, "Ashley, come in here this minute! Where have you been?"

A look of fright came over Ashley. "Only out walking."

"All this time!" Laura Anne was like a mother who finds out her daughter is safe and then wants to paddle her for giving her a scare.

Ashley burst into tears.

"Laura Anne and Zachary, you're upset. Why not let me handle this? May I speak with Ashley alone for a few minutes?" I spoke firmly. In my opinion, neither parent was calm enough to handle this situation appropriately.

"No, you may not," Laura Anne sputtered.

Zachary gripped Laura Anne's arm and turned her firmly toward the door.

"I'm not going anywhere, Zachary Taylor."

"Yes you are. Jennifer's a counselor. We're both leaving and letting someone professional deal with Ashley right now."

Laura Anne held back, "Ashley, are you okay?"

"Yes, mum." Her tears subsided.

"Alright." To my surprise, Laura Anne finally let Zachary pull her away. That may have been a first.

I turned to Ashley as soon as they left. "Sit down, honey."

She dutifully complied.

"This is a confusing time for you, isn't it?"

"Yes." She perched on the edge of the bed. Poor thing looked like a cardboard image of a girl. Her eyes were lowered.

"It can seem overwhelming to think about living with someone you're just getting to know. Is that why you left?"

I waited to see if I was on the right track, but Ashley said nothing.

"And leaving your Mom. Even though you weren't together that much, you're used to her, and going away is hard." Putting my arm around her shoulder, I asked, "Is that right?"

"Yes," she answered guardedly.

"Were you trying to run away?"

"No."

"Did you just want your parents to worry about you? Sometimes that's how kids act out to get more attention."

"I don't know."

"Did it make you feel more loved when you saw their concern?"

"Maybe, I wanted them to worry, I guess."

"Children often do things like this. Sometimes they think it will bring their parents closer. Would you like that?"

Ashley got a faraway look as if she'd disappeared into a memory only she could see. Who says kids can't remember certain events at one and two years of age? Ashley's sweet and guileless expression made my mama's heart sick. Once again, she didn't answer.

"It rarely does..."

"What?" she asked, returning her focus to me.

"Bring them together."

"Oh." She sighed.

"There's something else we should discuss. I want to assure you. You're going to love living in America with your daddy."

Ashley's eyes showed some light at last. "He's kind," she said.

"You'll be very happy. The schools are wonderful. And the city you'll live in is very nice." I said "very" twice using my most positive tone.

A spring rain of tears pattered Ashley's cheeks, then a deluge. Her words stammered forth finally. "I almost left. I walked and I walked, but I couldn't." Ashley spoke between sniffles. I wrapped her thin shoulders in a big hug.

"Good. Your daddy wants you and loves you very, very much. If you feel scared about anything again, will you promise to come talk with me before you do anything else?"

Ashley hiccupped, then softly she said, "Yes."

Glasses of Riesling, beef brisket flanked by golden onions, potatoes and glazed carrots. Only slivers remained as remnants of our hearty meal. A bouquet of pink roses sat in the center of our Glendale Restaurant table. Laura Anne said she'd made reservations there because of its convenient location next door to our Bed and Breakfast.

The floral fragrance mingled with scents of Earl Grey tea. The dinner guests, eight besides our group, were passing around petit fours frosted with buttercream. We devoured them, then watched as two servers cleared the table and efficiently served our coffee.

Laura Anne chattily made small talk with us and the other guests.

"I could definitely get used to this kind of luxury," I joked to Zachary.

Jenny overheard. "I agree, mom, no more setting the table or dishes for me."

Zachary leaned back in his chair and draped his arm across the back of Ashley's. In this particular moment a serene look of total contentment flashed across his face and made me smile.

The girls excused themselves to sit at another table and play a card game.

"Nice as this has been in many ways," I said, "I miss my husband Nick. I'm glad he'll be back tomorrow night to finalize things. Then we can get your papers signed and be on our way. I confess I'm eager to resume my normal routine, as unpredictable as that can be at times." I laughed.

"But you're pleased you accepted my request to come?" Zachary asked.

"Definitely, happy I could be here to assist you and Ashley. Besides, traveling anywhere with Nick, the love of my life, and my precious Jenny is pure joy."

"I can understand that." He smiled. "I'm amazed how much I've missed Lydia. I'm eager to introduce her to Ashley when the time is right."

"Step by step," I cautioned.

CHAPTER TEN

The next morning the significance of Zachary and Ashley's relationship temporarily faded into the background.

I received a call at eight A.M., from the White Rose Bed and Breakfast staff to come immediately to their first floor office. Mystified, I threw on a bathrobe and complied. Inside the living room, two police officers stood beside the elderly couple who ran the establishment. The owners were seated and looked none too happy. Laura Anne and Zachary arrived right after me. The three of us stood in a semi-circle.

"Sadly we're here to share some bad news," the tallest of the two officers began.

"What is it now?" Laura Anne sounded annoyed at being awakened early. "Did Ashley run off again?" She appeared more angry than concerned.

The officer said, "Don't know nothin' bout that, Ma'am, you might want to sit down and brace yourself. Regretfully, and I apologize, there's no easy way to say this, but we need to inform you that your husband, the Duke of Wycham, is dead. I'm very sorry to bring you this information." He paused. "The Duke opened a package yesterday containing a bomb which exploded in his hands, killing him instantly."

Laura Anne gasped and crumpled onto the nearest chair. The officer's words left us all speechless. "I'm sorry to intrude on your trip, but you need to return to Wycham Castle immediately. Our detective wishes to question you Mrs. Wycham and your traveling party as well. We had a delay tracking you down because you hadn't shared your destination with anyone except your deceased husband. Sorry it took us so long."

Zachary erupted with anger, fueled undoubtedly by stress. "What are you saying? I mean it's a horrid thing, but why interrogate us? How can you think we could possibly be suspects? We were nowhere near when this occurred."

The officer assumed an indifferent tone. "An explosive device sent by mail doesn't rule anyone out. But let's not jump ahead. I said 'question' not 'accuse'. You, Zachary Taylor, the Duke's wife and Mr. and Ms. Trevor are persons of interest. You were with him shortly before he died."

Laura Anne remained speechless. She appeared numb, perhaps in shock, and didn't seem capable of responding.

I gazed at her compassionately and said, "I'll make the arrangements for our return, Laura Anne."

Silently she nodded agreement. For the first time in my presence, Laura Anne willingly relinquished control. She gave me the number of Richard, her lawyer brother-in-law, and went to her room to dress.

I rang the manor and organized plans for our return trip.

Alone in our room I dropped onto the bed and prayed. "Jesus, my first concern is poor George's soul. He'd sounded so arrogant and unreachable when we dined together. May he have had a change of heart about You before he died!"

When all the details for our travel were in place, I went to the door of Laura Anne's suite and tapped a steady beat on the door.

Minutes later she opened, her hair tousled, eyes wide.

"Sorry, I must have startled you. I didn't mean to."

Her eyes glimmered like green pinpoints.

"Would you like to talk before we head out? Maybe I could be of help..."

"Not likely, Jennifer, unless you can glue me together. Isn't that what counselors do? I feel as if I'm coming apart." She dramatized her words by squeezing her forearms together.

I drew close and put my arms around her in a gentle hug. She stiffened, evidently not accustomed to physical touch. I backed off.

That there could be yet another bomb reverberated through my brain as we prepared to rush back. I wished Nick had already returned from his golf excursion. How ironic. A bomb explodes in a movie, and we sit on the edge of our seat and call it entertainment. In real life, it's terrifying.

I said gently to Laura Anne, "The limo will be here soon to take us to the train. The B & B has provided sandwiches and fruit to eat on the way."

"This can't be true, Jennifer. A bomb! No way! George can't be dead!" Her voice shrieked. "It doesn't make sense. Who would do such a thing?"

Of course, I had no answer. I offered my sincere condolences again, even as I observed her reaction.

Her shock seemed real, but then how did I know if she were a skilled actress? I noticed she never said "my" George or "my" husband, but kept repeating, "It can't be..."

Her fists clenched "I don't know what to do. I have to tell Ashley. Could you tell her for me? I don't want to break down in front of her. She must be returned to school immediately."

"Of course. You don't have to do anything, Laura Anne. Let me help you collect your things."

When I went to inform Zachary about the timing for our departure, he said, "How awful! I'm sorry for Duke George and whatever trouble brought this on. Still, I can't help but wonder how this will affect Ashley and me."

His reaction didn't surprise me. No doubt where Zachary's priorities were. Totally understandable.

"Depending on the relationship Ashley and her step-dad shared, which I haven't been able to assess yet, his death may be not be too traumatic for her."

"I hope not. Where's Ashley now?"

"In her room with Jenny still asleep. Laura Anne asked me to tell Ashley about her step-father. She said she couldn't bear to. I'm waiting for the girls to wake up."

"Figures. Laura Anne never was emotionally strong. I'll go with you."

I lowered my head and said softly, "Often psychological strength is a byproduct of spiritual strength which needs to come first."

"Tell me about it. My life story revolved around a family background of alcoholism. With God's help and lots of personal effort I survived. Thank God for my faith now."

"Since the rest of our trip must be cancelled, Laura Anne says she'll discuss custody later. Sorry to be the bearer of this news."

Zachary groaned, "I know I'm being selfish, but I don't want to go back to the castle unless I can take Ashley with me."

"I'm sorry Zachary, but Laura Anne insists Ashley be returned to school temporarily and we must return to the castle. You heard the police. The inspector heading the investigation wants to question each of us."

"How absurd," he said. Yet he sounded worried.

"After all, we were with Duke George the day before he died. I'm sure it's just routine."

Zachary accompanied me to the girls' room to tell his daughter about her stepfather, since Laura Anne had given me the task.

"I don't know how she'll take this." Zachary rubbed his palms together. "Poor girl, I wanted to bring her only happy news."

"You don't have to be in on this."

"No, I need to be there for her in hard times and good. I want to be an emotionally connected dad."

Ashley opened the door. "Jenny's in the shower."

"That's okay. We came to speak with you, honey," I said.

I related the event as gently as I could, but still Ashley hid her head in her hands at the news. No sobbing, only silence ensued. I had no way of knowing if she was upset out of fondness for her stepfather or just the horror of such an event. I realized this might well be her first experience with death.

Tenderly, Zachary put his hand on his daughter's shoulder and pulled her against him. "I'm so sorry, sweetie. Please know I'm here for you, whatever you need."

His words were kind and comforting. Ashley had no response other than clinging to him.

This wasn't the time for discussing her feelings. That would come later.

Finally, reassured Ashley was coping as best she could, Zachary left to pack for our return. I stayed behind with Ashley.

Her first teary-eyed words to me when we were alone surprised me. "I knew something bad would happen. Nothing ever goes right for me!"

Surprised, I stared at her. Ashley was concerned her stepfather's death might interfere with Zachary's plans for taking her to America? I didn't expect such a self-centered reaction as if her step-father meant nothing to her. I'd sensed she was a caring person.

Jenny came in, hugged Ashley after she heard the news and then looked up at me with uncertainty in her eyes. "What happens now?"

I hugged Jenny and Ashley tightly and told them that Laura Anne had insisted Ashley return to school immediately. "Jenny, can you please stay with Ashley until her nanny arrives. You don't have to say or do anything. Being there with her will help."

Ashley started to cry. "I don't want to go back."

"Oh, Mommy, it's so sad. Now she has to go."

"I know, sweetie. Our time with Ashley was too brief, but God willing we'll see her in America."

I hid my frustration. I had tried to persuade Laura Anne to let Ashley stay. "Psychologically it's much healthier to let your daughter participate in the burial arrangements," I'd explained.

Laura Anne was adamant. "I don't want Ashley exposed to the concept of death at her young age."

I could see why Zachary had a relationship problem with his former wife. It wasn't easy to communicate with a block of concrete.

Before we boarded the train for our return to the castle, Laura Anne threw us a crumb. "I'll consider signing over custodial rights to Zachary when all this is settled."

"Good," I answered immediately. "We need to be on the British Airways plane heading to the States with her by Monday."

"I know," she said, automatically, while appearing understandably distracted. "Right now, George's death is my priority."

How I wished I could trust Laura Anne to do the right thing.

CHAPTER ELEVEN

On our return ride for the most part everyone remained silent, processing their own thoughts.

When we arrived at the castle, the scene was chaos. Reporters and TV cameras were clustered in small groups. A team was filming the blackened skeleton remains of the western section of the castle. The media rushed toward our car, but British police held them back. We ignored their shouted questions as we hurried past.

Once within her home, Laura Anne immediately removed herself to her bedroom wing. Jenny lost herself in reading. I had no words to comfort Zachary, so I simply prayed silently.

The afternoon sun finished warming the earth for the day, and darkness had descended when we gathered in the living room at Wycham Manor.

Outdoors a sudden wind dragged the ensuing grayness from the sky and scattered it across the grounds. We heard the wind's plaintive moaning which accentuated the sadness we felt. A big part of something once beautiful had been desecrated, and with it a life lost.

I'd have preferred a seat in the chilly garden to this indoor gathering of servants, residents of the manor, and the inspector we'd just met. Every person in the immediate family was present except Ashley, who was already back at school. Laura Anne appeared subdued.

Inspector Blakely, a chunky man who chewed nonstop on an unlit cigar, took charge. Pausing between chomps he demanded of Laura Anne, "Please explain what you all were doing in Scotland, and why Duke George stayed behind?"

It surprised me that the inspector didn't want to question each of us privately. Perhaps they did things differently in England. Or he may have wanted to watch the reactions each person displayed.

"It's a bit complicated–" Laura Anne began and stopped abruptly, probably because it was a lot to explain. She hadn't even discussed the reasoning behind her demanding arrangement with Zachary much with us despite my efforts to get her to talk about it.

I hoped she wasn't going to bring up my role immediately. This whole affair had unsettled me. My experience with detectives had been limited in the past to Inspector Jarston in the States, who became a friend of sorts, depending on his mood at the moment. Jarston was vague and obtuse in his conversation in contrast to the bluntness of Inspector Blakely. Although, I quickly got the impression that Blakely's mouth possibly worked faster than his brain.

Nick had returned and met me at the castle. He sat at my side on the overstuffed sofa. The Inspector turned to him. "Why don't you tell me what's going on? I understand you're a lawyer."

Nick cleared his throat. No one, lawyer or not, likes being quizzed by law enforcement authorities. My husband explained the circumstances that had brought us together. Blakeley harrumphed, as if proclaiming how weird people can get.

Blakeley's assistant had already asked about our age, occupation and personal questions most of which were irrelevant and an invasion of privacy, but not worth making a scene over. From time to time, Blakeley looked down at the data he'd collected thus far from the interrogation sheet. If Blakeley had a deeper purpose with this information, it eluded me.

Finally, to my relief, he said, "Trevors, you're free to leave on Monday, but keep yourself available until then if I have more questions. Mr. Taylor, I need to quiz you further. You must admit, it's peculiar you being here the week Duke George Wycham died."

Zachary exploded. "I didn't come to England to commit murder, if that's what you're implying. I was supposed to be getting full custody of my daughter and the Duke seemed OK with it."

"No need to get upset, Mr. Taylor, unless of course you have something to hide." Blakeley tapped his unlit cigar against his open fist. "After all, you are the most logical suspect. If you came to get your wife and daughter back, what a convenient solution to dispose of her husband.'

Nick confided aside to me in a low voice, "Poor Zachary."

"True, this is hard on Zachary's self-concept considering his delicate emotional state," I murmured back.

"What's that, Dr. Trevor? Whatever you and your husband have to say, I'd like to hear it."

Nick answered for us. "Certainly, Inspector, I was stating how upsetting these circumstances are for my client Mr. Taylor who hired me to represent him during this change of custody. I'd appreciate if you'd not make baseless assumptions."

That was a bold thing to say but appropriate and typical for my husband.

"I agree." I added, trying to keep my tone polite.

My graciousness didn't work. The Inspector turned his verbal guns on me. "Are you willing to bend rules to help a counseling client, Mrs., excuse me, Dr. Trevor? These questions are essential to a thorough investigation. I hope you don't mind."

I bristled at his sarcastic tone.

Inspector Blakeley instantly added for emphasis, "You should know that, unless you're implicated in this too."

My face warmed like a torch. "I'm actually here in a consultant role, not as a personal counselor." My tone switched from polite to annoyed. "Why would any of us send George Wycham a mail bomb?" We hardly knew the man. I never saw him before two nights ago!"

"Now, now, don't get touchy." Blakeley undoubtedly sensed the irritation in my voice. "I understand indirectly Mr. Taylor had a very colorful history with the deceased."

Jenny had listened wordlessly to Blakeley's bellowing. In her sweetest manner, she said, "My mom's a psychotherapist and a detective, too. She solves murders, Inspector, she doesn't do them. She can help you solve this crime, if you let her."

"Quiet, darling!" I piped in. Still, I felt proud that my sweet daughter spoke up on my behalf.

"What's that?" Blakeley's eyes peered at me like a conductor suddenly seeing an orchestra member he'd ignored. "So you're one of those snoopy types I've seen on TV shows?"

What was that supposed to mean? I chose not to comment. Nick took up my banner next. He winked at me as he described for Blakeley my two past investigations in the Lenora Lawrence and Albert Windemere cases.

The Inspector studied me with a new kind of attentiveness that almost seemed like respect. "I must say I'm impressed."

"In truth," I said, "Windemere's murderer discovered me and almost killed me. However, my family still thinks I'm a heroine." I spoke with more than a modicum of modesty.

Blakeley said magnanimously, "Well, I'm not opposed to having a woman help if she's capable. I know the Federal Bureau of Investigation uses personality data in their research on criminal behavior. What's that place they do that? Teeko?"

"Quantico in Virginia," I clarified.

"Whatever," he harrumphed.

"I'd be happy to assist any way I can Inspector. Since you're inviting my involvement, may I ask, have there been any other recent mail bombings? Could there be any indication George's bomb was sent by a serial killer? Since you mentioned the FBI site, you probably know their work started as a way to catch serial killers by identifying common traits. "

"I'm not aware of any others as of now, but you can be assured we're checking this from every angle." Blakeley pointed his head in my direction. "You may come with me to view Duke George Wycham's den, the scene of this dastardly act."

"Certainly, I'll help any way I can."

Blakeley directed his next gaze at Laura Anne. "First, any former friend of your husband who might have turned an enemy, come into your mind?"

"George didn't have many friends."

"Not the social type?"

"He wasn't the kind of person who needed to be surrounded with people, although he was cordial and had buddies at the golf course where he was a member," Laura Anne offered.

"Thank you." Blakeley nodded toward his assistant who made a note of her answer.

Laura Anne added, "Whatever Zachary said, you need to question the person with the best motive. That's him!" Laura Anne stabbed her finger in Zachary's direction.

"What? Are you out of your mind, Laura Anne?" Zachary exploded. "How absurd. I wouldn't be surprised if you hadn't arranged this entire event to implicate me."

The Inspector watched their verbal exchange with interest.

"Mr. Taylor, all the same, I do need you to stick around for further questioning. Relax. You're not being arrested. Yet."

Blakeley turned to Nick and me. "In fact, I'd like you all to stay until I've finished the preliminary investigation, which hopefully will be by the weekend. I don't think Laura Anne would mind putting you up a little longer under the circumstances. Appears to be plenty of room here and quite habitable except for the wing damaged by the bomb. And after all she did invite you as guests, didn't she?"

Laura Anne frowned but didn't reply.

"Thank you, Inspector," I agreed. "The sooner we get to the truth about what happened here, the better."

I needed to make sure Blakeley didn't mischaracterize Zachary's involvement. My role would be protecting his interests and promoting his innocence.

"You're all under suspicion at present. We haven't ruled out the possibility of the murderer having accomplices in this."

"Oh great!" Zachary fumed. He turned to Laura Anne "We need to complete the custody papers quickly."

"We'll discuss that when I'm ready." Laura Anne whipped orders to her maid regarding our rooms.

I inserted my professional recommendation. "It would be wise to get Ashley out of the country as soon as possible. She could be in danger, and you as well. Who knows the motive for this bomb?"

"At present, Zachary, giving you Ashley is the furthest thing from my mind and may not even happen. I need to rethink everything."

"But you said–" Zachary blurted out.

Nick put an arm on Zachary's shoulder to restrain him. Quietly he said, "Let's give her a little time."

Laura Anne stalked off following an admonition from the inspector to be prepared for the possibility of more questions.

"Dr. Trevor, I'll take you with me to see the bomb site now," Blakely said.

"Yes, please."

Nick stayed behind with Zachary to calm his concern.

We went down the long hallway past a bobbie guarding the entry. Yellow crime scene tape delineated the ruins.

Nothing in my past life prepared me for the shock of the destruction before me.

CHAPTER TWELVE

I forced my body to stop gaping and continue walking forward into what once had been Duke George's magnificent office. The mail bomb had blown a huge hole in the eighteen-foot-high ceiling. The intricate stained-glass window on the side wall had exploded into shrapnel. Duke George's glasses, scorched and crackled had shot through the air and landed in a corner where they remained now. I shuddered at the black hole where Duke George had sat. The poor man's body remnants, what they'd been able to collect of them, had already been removed.

I stepped sideways, cautious of debris on my path, to study the opening where the window had been. Questions seared through my brain. Had the bomb exploded as planned? Had the intent been to destroy the entire castle? Or was the bomb only for Duke George? Where I stood, a section of the wall had caved to the ground.

The inspector made general comments. "I had the area cordoned off immediately as a crime scene."

Plastic tape stretched around the entire area. Just as well, the debris appeared quite dangerous.

I wished I hadn't seen the vestiges of this disaster. It was the stuff of nightmares.

Nevertheless, I held up my phone. 'May I take pictures?"

"Photographs have been taken of every detail, but don't suppose more would hurt." Gazing intently at me, Blakeley asked, "Have you had any experience with a scene like this?"

"No. You?"

Before he answered, I read the answer in his eyes.

"I wish I could be more helpful Inspector."

"Fortunately we have someone who may be." He gestured toward a bomb expert dressed in a khaki uniform examining and collecting refuse.

We approached him.

"Almost done here. As you may know, residues of explosives can be analyzed and classified for types, but most are difficult to identify as to source. I'll get back to you with a formal report soon. These despicable homemade bombs create horrible devastation," he announced with a shake of his head.

I had a sudden thought. "Are you sure these are the remains of the Duke of Wycham? I understand no one was here to see him open the package."

"Good thought, Ms. Trevor, but thankfully we salvaged dental proof and already have clothing fragments." The expert added, "Blood, semen, sweat, urine, saliva, and other fluids are used to confirm DNA identity in investigations, but tough to get after a bombing. DNA can take typically around two to four weeks for the twenty-one marker genetic analysis. Of course we'll check dental records in more detail, but I'm confident my finding is conclusive. The Duke opened the package."

"No one else had access to this area other than employees," Blakeley announced. "Interviewing staff is next, Ms. Trevor. Perhaps you can provide insight with that. Follow me."

Dawson the chauffeur was located and brought into the sitting area off the formal living room. The ruddy-faced man, tall and lanky, fiddled continually with his cap. His thick brown hair was disheveled as if he'd been running his hand through it repeatedly.

"Sorry you couldn't reach me sooner, Inspector. Today's my day off. After I gave my report last night, I took off to see my mum. She gets upset if I'm not there at visiting time."

Blakely made no response to his excuse. "You're here now. Sit down."

The cook, Alicia, was escorted into the room by Blakeley's assistant.

Blakeley snapped orders. “Go to the sofa and wait. I want details from you all about the afternoon this box was delivered.”

In bits and pieces Dawson described what he knew. “It musta been left on the porch. I never saw a delivery van. Dawson shuddered and stopped for a breath.

“Continue,” Blakeley insisted.

The cook inserted, “The Duke ate his lunch, orange juice, a fried egg sandwich and fruit like usual, then I saw him head in the direction of his office wing. It was a quiet day, not much activity around the castle with the duchess gone.” Then, well you know the rest.”

“Yes, you were the first to enter the Duke’s area, correct, Dawson?”

“That’s right. I ran to where the sound came from. At the front of the opening where the door had been, I stepped into a dark mass. The electricity was out. The Duke may have yelled, nobody heard. Shreds of building material were falling to the ground like a shower of pelting rain. The room had ignited like a paper box. A wall of fire, metal, burning boards spewing ashes everywhere. I sensed immediately the Duke was gone. No one could survive that. I sprinted out, fearing for my life, and called 911. You know the rest.”

The cook said, “I heard Dawson yell and dashed to the hall. A wave of heat rolled at my legs. Then I ran to the front door and screamed. Yeah, I know that was foolish. No neighbors are close enough to hear me.”

Blakeley jotted down a few notes before he dismissed them from the sitting room.

Then he turned to me. "The maid Valerie, Dawson's wife, became hysterical when it happened and was heavily sedated. Only just recently is she coherent."

She was escorted in next.

With typical English formality Valerie sat primly in her neat uniform. Her short auburn hair, visible from strands around her face, had blonde streaks.

I sometimes envy uniform-wearers. I often find I have too many choices of clothing in my closet. Silly thought. I refocused on Valerie. She acted demure, but her eyes glinted with hardness. Which is why I had to question whether her sweetness was an act.

The household staff must have known there was tension between the Duke and his wife. Hard to fool people under the same roof who observe you daily. I wondered, did the maid side with her master or mistress?

I listened to Blakeley's questions without comment, grateful that he allowed me to sit in.

"How long have you been employed at Wycham Manor?"

"Three years."

Blakeley's silent sidekick wrote down her answers as he'd done before.

"Valerie, I understand delivering the mail was your role."

"Yes, Sir. I took it in around one each day."

"Did the Duke often get packages?"

"Yes, sir. He often ordered books. An avid reader he was." She added the last part with a modicum of pride. I sensed that she admired him.

"Describe what you saw when you brought yesterday's mail in, ma'am."

"Same as usual. Who knew that I carried contained a bomb? Blimey, it could have gone off while I held it! I did what I always do with mail and packages. I brought it to Duke George's den office and left it on the right side of the big desk where he liked me to put stuff."

"Was the Duke present at the time?"

"He was sitting behind his desk looking at his phone."

"The box was right on top?"

"Yes, sir."

"Did you have any conversation with the Duke?"

"Nothing outside of the ordinary." Valerie blushed.

A relationship with him? I filed that away to think through later.

"Did you happen to notice a Royal Mail truck on the premises yesterday or any other delivery service?"

"No sir."

"Tell me more about the box. Can you describe it?"

"A carton about the size of a large shoe box."

"And the wrapping?"

"It was wrapped simply in brown paper."

"Was there a string?"

"No, I don't think so. Seems to me it'd been taped shut. But I can't be sure about that."

"Can you describe the label?

"Yes, I remember that clearly."

"Go on."

She swiped her hand across her forehead. "Well I wasn't being nosy, but I couldn't help but notice there was no proper return address, just a Go To label."

Blakely turned to me. "Any other questions, Dr. Trevor?"

"When you say, 'there was no regular return' you mean the space was blank?" I asked. "Most shipping companies want the return filled in."

"I mean it was cause the address written on the 'From part' was the same as the 'Go To' mailing address. Either way the package would've come to us."

"You're sure about this?"

She hesitated.

I was forcing her to admit she'd been intrusive, which a maid wouldn't like to do.

Valerie tossed her head back. "Yes, I'm an observant woman."

Our eyes met and she looked away.

"I can tell," I said. "Thank you."

Inspector Blakeley, after several more questions, dismissed her with a wave of his hand saying, "That's all for now."

After she'd gone, I turned to the Inspector. "I assume you've already run a trace through the mail system?"

"Of course. No record of this delivery. Either there was a slip-up in recording or more likely this package was hand-delivered and left with the daily mail."

"Unless Valerie's lying and someone handed it to her at the door. I imagine you're looking into the possibility of her having had a personal relationship with the Duke?"

Blakeley's grey-blue eyes brightened. They were the most lively thing about his otherwise sluggish appearance. "Hmm. I'm not prepared to think that yet, but I suppose it's worth checking out."

"I only bring it up because I deal in human behavior. A woman scorned in a romantic relationship is capable of inflicting great harm."

Blakeley grunted. "Rotten business, despicable method of murder, as if any is okay. But a woman might find a bomb more to her liking than a pistol. Still, we're doing a thorough check on every employee's background. Zachary Taylor's too."

He didn't have to add yours too, but I could guess that from the way he looked at me. Lord, how do I get involved in these situations?

"Inspector, if we're through for now, I'd like to get back to my husband and daughter."

"I'll want to talk to your group again after dinner, especially Mr. Taylor, your client. We've explored his family history, which frankly doesn't look stable."

"His lawyer, my husband, will vouch for his character. Of course, we'll be available."

The moment I left him, I desperately craved quiet and privacy to sort out my thoughts on this horror.

I mourned for Duke George and for all of us. Death, especially premature death, is always tragic. Only God should have power over human life. I'd seen horror in war movies like this.

Once in the bedroom I'd stayed in previously, I closed my eyes to fight these images and tried to nap. After twenty minutes, I shook my head and gave up. Sleep would come later hopefully, but not now. My emotions overpowered me. "Oh God," I said aloud. My eyes filled with tears. I swiped them away and pushed myself to a standing position. I had to focus on helping Zachary.

Get a grip, Jennifer.

CHAPTER THIRTEEN

By late evening Blakely had finished preliminary questioning, and his behind-the-scenes research apparently was proceeding rapidly. Every individual had been checked out thoroughly, at least I hoped that was true.

Laura Anne, Zachary and my family dined together on cold beef and chicken sandwiches and chips in what was usually the breakfast room. The cook had been relieved of further duties today.

"It's all off for now, of course." Laura Anne's golden locks, twisted into a barrette, swung casually from side to side.

I saw Zachary flinch like someone had delivered a dagger puncturing his heart.

Laura Anne continued. "Until I'm sure, Zachary, that you're not involved in my husband's death, there's no way I'll give you custody of Ashley. I must protect my daughter."

His face turned red.

I interceded quickly. "Laura Anne, think how preposterous that would be. If Zachary wanted to murder your husband with a mail bomb, he could have done it any time these last eight years from Chicago, Illinois. He wouldn't have waited until he was actually on the scene and finally getting custody of his daughter. Why do anything to jeopardize that?"

She balked. "How do I know if meeting Duke George in person for the first time didn't trigger tremendous anger in him? Although Zachary may have wanted to destroy the Duke all along for stealing my affection and didn't know how to pull it off before."

"So you think Zachary's so-called obsession with your past affair led to killing him in this fantasy you've conjured up." I couldn't keep the sarcasm out of my voice.

"Seeing my lifestyle and contentment now could have gnawed at him."

Zachary faked a laugh. "You always did overestimate yourself. I was over you weeks after you left."

Laura Anne whipped around toward me. "Don't you understand? If I'm right, now he gets Ashley and accomplishes revenge at the same time."

"I know how upset you are, Laura Anne, but I hope you're able to comprehend rational argument. Let's be logical. How would Zachary know that your husband would open his own mail? He'd likely assume he had a secretary responsible for it. Actually I'm surprised Duke George didn't."

Laura Anne shot back, "He insisted on being the only one who touched his mail. It was sacrosanct! All the servants knew that. Zachary could have found out from them somehow."

I shook my head. "Rather far-fetched."

"You don't know what cruelty Zachary is capable of. I do." She hurled the accusation at me. "It's only two weeks since you first met him! I know because he told me." She pulled a nail file out of her purse and began sawing a nail like Paul Bunyan felling a tree. "I know him very well."

Zachary, to his credit, ignored her hurtful words and focused on his daughter. "I insist on Ashley coming back here for the weekend so I can at least see her again if you won't let her come home with me."

Laura Anne snarled like a sheep dog warding off a bear attacking her cub. She rolled her eyes. "Don't you care anything about Ashley's feelings? Seeing the castle devastated by the bomb would be too traumatic. Ashley must be protected emotionally from this horror."

"I understand and intend to do exactly that. I can get lodging for us in town."

"No, and that's my final answer." She turned as if to leave, but I laid my hand on her arm.

"Laura Anne, just so you know, it's not realistic to think you can guard your child from any trauma in life. Some will simply be an inevitable part of growing up."

"May I remind you, Ms. Trevor, that you have three children, and I only have one. And I intend to guard my daughter."

My breath sped up, and I felt my stomach tensing. Time to throw caution to the wind. At this point we had nothing to lose. "If I may make a comment, Laura Anne. You personally don't seem extremely devastated by your husband's death."

Zachary chimed in, "Yeah! How do we know you didn't arrange this whole thing? The timing of our visit was planned by you. Perhaps you and the Duke were having marital issues. This visit made us a perfect set-up to take the blame."

"The Duke was deeply in love with me. We lived in separate wings, but..."

I interrupted her. "Excuse me. I've heard of separate rooms, but separate wings?"

"Duke George and I had a wonderful relationship. Over the years we became less intimate, that's all. You know how reserved the English are. True, he could be rather difficult at times, but I knew how to deal with him."

"I bet you did." Zachary shot her a disgusted look.

"Zachary," she retorted, "What would you know about the way royalty lives?"

"Another totally arrogant statement as usual!" It slipped out of Zachary's mouth, and he immediately seemed sheepish. He may have regretted it the minute he spoke the words. He looked at me. I raised and rolled my hand slightly like an orchestra conductor calming the musicians' tone. I hoped he'd see that as a gesture to go easier. At least until the papers for Ashley's custody were signed.

Zachary recovered his manners quickly and said, "Laura Anne, you're right, it's not been my life experience."

I decided to be careful around this volatile woman. I doubted she could take word warfare as well as she gave it to others. I changed the topic. "Did you and the Duke have many common interests?"

Laura Anne responded quickly, too fast in my opinion. "The Duke's investment work was all-consuming. He required considerable time alone and I respected his privacy." She pulled out a Kleenex. Close to tears or pretending?

As long as Laura Anne was allowing me to ask questions, I immediately posed another. "Did Duke George have a close relationship with Ashley? Or was she a disturbance to his work and quiet lifestyle?"

Not surprisingly Laura Anne had a pat answer ready. "The majority of his work was done in his office from his leather desk chair which he loved. The arrival of Ashley hadn't changed his style or routine. In fact, he handled the adjustment well in a noble, gentlemanly fashion. We had a clear understanding. My daughter was my responsibility. As long as we could be together, he was fine with whatever. The Duke didn't take an interest in matters that didn't concern him." Laura Anne turned the subject away from Duke George as fast as she could, then immediately excused herself.

Once again her will regarding Zachary's contact with Ashley prevailed.

Later when Zachary, Nick and I were alone, Nick said, "I wouldn't be surprised if Duke George wasn't secretly happy that Ashley would be restored to her legitimate father and out of his domain."

"That could be true," I responded. "Duke George certainly didn't seem overly concerned about Ashley's departure for America. At least he never referred to it during our dinner together."

Zachary shrugged. Changing the subject he said, "I thought I got on rather well with Duke George overall in the limited time we had together."

"True, which is what I'd expect. You said back in the States, you and George never had angry words. When you arrived in London, his behavior toward you was fairly cordial. During our dinner, I didn't get the impression that Duke George disliked you at all."

"That's what I surmised," Nick said.

"Thanks for your support," Zachary said. "I can't tell you how grateful I am for your presence here." He rose. "I'm going for a walk in the rain. It matches my mood. See you later."

I sighed softly. Through the window I stared at trickles of rain released by low hanging clouds. How distant the sun was at night, yet how predictably its rays, returning even after having been totally hidden from human vision for a long time.

"Nick, what a bizarre thought that Zachary could have done this? Why does Laura Anne continue to push that? I refuse to believe it. True, I've known him less than two weeks, but I've counseled enough clients over the years to trust my instincts about people."

"I totally agree, but who did?"

That became the refrain that played non-stop in my brain the rest of the day.

I appreciated Laura Anne's offer to have Jenny supervised by Ashley's nanny who lived nearby and offered to come over daily. There must be a kind streak in Laura Anne somewhere. Knowing Jenny was well cared for freed me up to help with the investigation and Nick might as well enjoy some more golf since there was nothing else pressing for him to do.

Laura Anne had made me feel at first that she wanted me to help discover who had killed her husband. But I wasn't sure this was her true emotion. Instead it might be a superficial gesture or a ploy to distract focus from her.

In our room later, Jenny tugged at my skirt, a cute reminder from when she was a toddler and wanted my attention. "Mommy, why can't I see Ashley now? She must be upset about her step-dad and the bomb."

"It's kind of you to be concerned, sweetie. Ashley's okay for now. She's in a familiar place. You, on the other hand, are blessed to enjoy more vacation time playing games with Ashley's kind nanny and reading."

Jenny grinned. "You're right. This is way more fun than school."

"I'm glad you're happy because we need to stay a few more days to try to help Mr. Taylor. Then hopefully Ashley can go back to America with him."

"Okay, but I do miss her. We were having lots of fun together. I'd do anything to help her and you, Mommy. I feel so sorry for her. Unless she can go home with Mr. Taylor, she has nobody except her mother who sometimes seems pretty mean."

I patted my daughter's head. "We mustn't judge, sweetie. Ashley's mom may think she's kind and fair and doing right by her daughter." I doubted that even as I spoke the words.

"Well, she's not. If you were like her, I couldn't stand it, Mom. And don't ever divorce Daddy, please!"

I wrapped my arms around Jenny's shoulders and squeezed her softly. "For sure, darling. Mommy and Daddy will always be together."

Jenny smiled, relieved, and ran off to play.

Sadness overwhelmed me that we had to drag our precious daughter through this. My only recourse at the moment was prayer.

I spoke aloud, "Lord, let this end well, please, and may we be on that plane Monday." My thoughts immediately went to Colin and Tara, my precious children back in the States. I wondered what they were doing at this very moment and missed them terribly.

CHAPTER FOURTEEN

Events took a dramatic turn for the worse the next morning. Inspector Blakeley arrived as our group was finishing breakfast. He lit into Zachary like an orchestra conductor building to a crescendo. "Someone noticed you hanging around Duke George's office after dinner the night you were here together? She says she overheard you having a private conversation with him afterwards. I'd like to know what you discussed."

"That's right. It was personal." Zachary shifted in his chair. "Who told you this, Inspector?" He turned his head Laura Anne's way. "This is the lowest thing you've ever done."

Blakeley intervened. "Under the circumstances, information like this cannot remain confidential, Mr. Taylor. You can appreciate that, surely."

"I've nothing to hide. I'll give you a little background first. In discussing the custody situation with Nick Trevor, my attorney, I got to thinking about my attitude toward Duke George all these years."

"Ahh!" I swear the Inspector licked his lips in anticipation.

"And I realized that I needed to apologize to him."

"Apologize?" The inspector's eyebrows pumped up and down like miniature dumbbells. "For what? Hadn't you been cuckolded by the Duke?"

I listened intently, suddenly curious.

Zachary continued, "Yes, and I realized I'd harbored bitterness against Duke George all these years. What happened was as much my wife's fault as his. Nick isn't just my lawyer. He's also a friend and Christian that I greatly respect. So when we discussed this..." Zachary paused and waved his arm in Nick's direction. "I saw some areas where I was wrong."

Nick injected, "That's true, we had several discussions about forgiveness."

Zachary continued. "I realized I needed to get my emotional accounting straight. In addition, Duke George and I discussed my finances. I assumed he'd be reassured to know I could provide well for Ashley. Truth is, seeing Laura Anne again made me feel sorry for him. She knows how to turn her charm off and on at a second's notice. And I couldn't blame either of them entirely for what happened. I wasn't the greatest husband."

Inspector Blakeley listened intently without interrupting. "What was Duke George's response to all this?"

"Shock, first of all. He didn't seem particularly interested in what I had to say about providing for Ashley. I got the impression he knew I would and didn't care very much either way about Ashley's presence. But he seemed taken aback by my apologizing to him."

"How do you know?"

"He insisted I elaborate. I explained that bitterness could be a heavy weight. I'd shoved my resentment to the back of my brain, but it ended up popping up and made me feel miserable every time I thought of him."

"Convenient explanation. However, I imagine the psychologist you're traveling with helped you come up with this. Now I want to know what you else talked about." The inspector's voice remained low, but menacing.

"That's all. I have nothing further to say. I can't make you believe me if you choose not to."

Blakeley stamped his foot. "Furthermore, it wasn't your ex-wife, but the maid Valerie who reported the comment she overheard you make. You referred to Duke George as the man you wanted to kill eight years ago. I see no reason to believe that your intentions changed."

"That's ridiculous!" Zachary snapped.

Blakeley harrumphed. "Nevertheless, based on that comment, I'm bringing you in for further questioning." Blakeley messaged for his assistant who shuffled into the room.

Zachary turned white. He made no effort to hide his fury.

Nick intervened immediately. "Relax. Zachary, we'll do all we can to clear this up. I'm going to find an excellent criminal lawyer immediately to help. Unfortunately, criminal law is not my specialty."

Zachary replied morosely. "I feel like I'm on an escalator that's gone out of control—when I feel stairs under me, they flatten out. Now look at the hell this woman has gotten me into."

Blakeley's sidekick led Zachary away.

Nick's neck vein bulged. His concern for Zach was obvious. "He's being sucked into this bombing based on circumstantial evidence."

"I know you're furious with what's happening. You and I don't get stressed often since becoming Christians because we release our problems to God and keep our joy and composure intact, but it's easier to do that with our own problems than with someone else we feel responsible for. Thank God Zachary has you to get him help. In the meantime, I'll keep investigating on my own to find out who really sent the bomb."

"Be careful." I read signals of distress in Nick's eyes. He didn't question my ability to ferret out information. His primary issue, I knew, was whether I could stay out of harm's way while I did.

Thoughts about stepfathers swirled in my brain. True, some were wonderful, but there was nothing like a real father's love for his daughter. Zachary exuded that whenever he mentioned Ashley's name. In my counseling it was my first intent to strengthen the paternal bond whenever possible. Yes, a real father could be emotionally distant, but that was far less likely to occur than with a stepfather.

Thinking about this relationship may have been why I chose to take my next drastic step.

I had no reason to enter Duke George's private bedroom wing. Yet I found myself moving in that direction. After all, Blakely had somewhat solicited my help. The hall was conveniently empty. I wanted to hurry but forced myself to walk at a normal pace. Someone might approach from the back stairway. The rubber bottoms of my Hoka tennies blunted the sound of my footsteps.

Laura Anne, I'd already observed, had left with Dawson, her chauffeur, to drive into town, ostensibly to handle insurance matters pertaining to the bomb damage. The servants appeared to be busy elsewhere. I'd encouraged Jenny to take a nap. As a result, I was left with nothing to do but explore. Who could resist?

I remembered which area was the Duke's from the maid's comments when we passed his bedroom wing on the day of our arrival. I assumed Laura Anne's wing was to the right of his. Certainly Inspector Blakeley had been in here, but I desired to look for myself. I feared the door would be locked, but the handle turned at my touch. I took a last, furtive glance down the hall, slipped my body through the doorway and released my breath inside.

Counselors don't do this sort of thing, but I wasn't counseling. I was consulting and helping a client accused of murder.

The room was totally dark. I turned on my phone flashlight. A stream of light hit the floor illuminating woven streaks of steel grey and maroon plaid on the carpet. I played the light in a circle around the room. My eyes gradually adjusted by dim light filtering through cracks in the thick burgundy drapes, and I shut off my phone torch. I saw grotesque outlines of giant-like tall furniture shapes. Drawing closer I saw they were antique bookshelves.

Before me was a softly lit short corridor leading to George's bathroom. I crept toward it, hunching my back to duck under the window. I didn't think my form could be seen through the drapes, but why risk it?

Inside the bath I took infinite care opening the medicine cabinet and drawers. Shaving supplies, deodorant, lotions, Tylenol P.M., a sleep aid. Nothing unusual. Then, on the bottom shelf behind a large bottle of mouthwash, I saw a prescription of Prozac.

Re-entering the bedroom area, I maneuvered my way toward the huge mahogany bed on a platform. Next to it, atop Duke George's night table, I noticed a small paper tablet. Picking it up, I flipped to the first page that had writing and stopped. A name J. Wilson and phone number had been hastily scribbled. I took a picture of it.

I still had my finger on my phone's camera when I heard voices rising to a crescendo. I froze as they came closer. The noise lowered after they passed. I exhaled. Sweat beads made my under arms sticky.

Suddenly the bedroom door opened, and a shaft of brightness entered. My reflexes jerked me instantly to the floor beside the bed.

Several seconds passed. I heard steps heading toward the bath. I lifted my head and dared a peek. The maid was walking toward the linen closet, her arms stacked with towels. She fumbled to open the door, single-handedly balancing the linens on her left thigh.

The next thing I knew, she left and the room dissolved into darkness again. I waited a bit, then pulled myself up and tiptoed to the door.

I closed my eyes to listen for any sound in the hall. Several minutes of silence passed before I twisted the door handle and gently pulled the door back on its hinges. I opened to about twelve inches, just enough to slide through.

Taking a deep breath, I headed for the stairs, grabbed the stair rail and propelled myself down, forcing myself not to skip a step. I passed the foyer where I saw the maid talking to the gardener. I strolled past at what I hoped was a natural pace toward the guest wing.

On the way, a small sane voice in my head accused me, "What are you doing sneaking around like this? How foolish and awkward as well. What if someone saw you?"

Another voice that I hoped was the Holy Spirit said, "You go, girl, and help this poor father get cleared of any wrongdoing."

CHAPTER FIFTEEN

Laura Anne had been notified by her brother-in-law, and her lawyer, Richard, that Duke George's personal will was intact and would be read immediately. To my surprise, we were invited to attend. Nick sat at my side.

Richard's wife, Constance, had accompanied him and sat nearby as we all assembled in the sitting room now doubling as a study. Richard remained standing. The hallway to the restoration area where the bomb damage occurred was blocked off.

Rosalind was present of course. She chose a chair next to Nick and me. I could smell her gardenia body scrub. Swirls of colorful flowers decorated her blouse, complementing a tasteful three-quarter length black skirt. Simple and elegant. Her taste always impressed me, but even more her gracious Christian demeanor. Had she lived near me in Wisconsin, I had a feeling we'd be good friends.

Richard said to the group by way of explanation regarding the speed of this process, "The Duke would want Laura Anne to get her life in order and move forward. Also we need to continue the family philanthropy projects which our local charities depend on. The settlement on the historical property itself will be forthcoming later."

Rosalind turned to me and said, "Laura Anne and Duke George were huge supporters of charities. I'm sure she's anxious to know if Duke George made arrangements for them." Strange, I thought, Zachary had given me the impression that Laura Anne's giving was more for social recognition than charitable intent. Whatever, at least the organizations benefited.

Constance must have overheard. "Generosity is a Wycham tradition. The Duke gave Laura Anne the privilege of distributing gifts."

Seems Duke George humored Laura Anne's whims well.

Laura Anne fluttered in a few minutes past two. She appeared not the least bit distressed at this solemn event. Frankly, I was still shocked at her easy acceptance of Duke George's death. If the inspector had been more alert to the absence of her grieving process, Laura Anne might have been more scrutinized early on as a suspect.

The maid Valerie and her husband, Dawson, as long-time servants, had been invited to be present. I presumed

Duke George had gifted them with a bequest. I'd heard the couple were in his employ many years.

I noticed Rosalind observing the group with a thoughtful expression. Her kind Christian spirit was evident in her conversation. I overheard her speak to Laura Anne in a tone of sweet sympathy. "How are you doing, dear?"

"Coping, just barely, I know losing a husband happens to many women sooner or later. Still, these horrendous circumstances make it extra hard. I know you'll say I must accept what I can't change. I'm trying." Laura Anne leaned my way. "Isn't that what counselors say, Jennifer?"

I half-smiled at her. "Sadly, Laura Anne, with all due respect, people mourn precisely because something has happened that they can't easily accept. Mourning is healthy as long as individuals don't get stuck and can't resume a normal life. Then again, the degree of difficulty of grief depends on the relationship the couple shared. Everyone mourns differently. "

Laura Anne threw her shoulders back. "I hope to move forward as quickly as I can."

"Good to hear. As Christians we have God's reassuring promise to comfort us." I tried to communicate sympathy, although I wasn't sure she truly needed it.

"Where is Mr. Taylor?" Rosalind inquired, suddenly noticing his absence.

Laura Anne answered. "He's been taken for questioning."

Rosalind looked like someone had shot an arrow into the room. “Laura Anne, you don’t for a second believe...”

Laura Anne turned her head. “Zachary’s a stranger to me after all these years. I have no way of knowing if he’s capable of such a thing. He may even have wanted us to open the package together.”

“Surely someone else must have sent the bomb!” Rosalind shook her head from side to side as if in disbelief.

“If not him, maybe....” Laura Anne looked at me sharply. I swear she changed her mind about what she was going to say next.

“I never heard whose name was on the package? I’d just assumed Duke George’s, correct?” I asked.

“No one’s, just Wycham Castle. But everybody around here knew the Duke opened the mail himself.” Laura Anne clarified. “He insisted.”

A click went off in my brain. Duke George must not have trusted his wife completely. Why else would he want to check all mail? I’ve observed that when a marriage dissolves because of a couple’s growing apart or outright deceit, it’s not uncommon for partners to be paranoid that their spouse has been unfaithful or is stealing their money.

Rosalind turned to Richard. “It’s possible the bomb was intended for you, isn’t it?”

Richard’s face turned the color of a turnip. He shrank into the nearest chair, a rocker. The sudden motion seemed to startle him.

"I mean you often worked in the office with him, correct?"

"It couldn't possibly be ..." Richard said, forcing a lighthearted tone.

Just then the inspector noisily entered through the door.

Laura Anne directed her attention to him. "Inspector Blakeley, this is a surprise." I noticed she didn't say pleasant. "Whatever are you doing here?"

"I came for the reading of the will. Duke George may have left me a gift." He smiled as if he'd made a clever, if inappropriate, joke. Definitely a sick sense of humor. "Why, wasn't I invited?"

"No need to summon you for something totally unrelated to the bombing event," she said pointedly. "I'm curious. How did you hear?"

"I found out from your chauffeur, Dawson, when I called to inquire about another matter."

Laura Anne's arms stiffened, but she didn't bother to look in Dawson's direction. If she had, I believe Dawson would have gotten something other than a smile.

Richard stood again and took control. "We're all present now. Let's proceed." Falling into his professional role, he displayed a sense of competence not visible in his prior social exchanges with us.

The will was dutifully read.

Laura Anne inherited an adequate amount of cash for her yearly sustenance. She huffed when she heard the bequest to their servants, obviously displeased. $10,000 gifts went to Valerie and Dawson providing they continued employment at the castle at least three more years. They would be allowed to retain their living privileges in an apartment above the garage as long as they wished.

Richard continued, "No mention is made yet about the disposition of the castle and land holdings due to more intricate legal issues about family ownership of the historical dukedom. That's all for now."

People stood to file out.

Blakeley motioned me toward a corner of the room. Evidently, he still trusted me as his fellow investigator. He confided, "Typically, I find British servants aren't inclined to talk, but Valerie seemed quite fond of Duke George. She didn't like the way Laura Anne treated him. In addition to badmouthing Zachary, she's verbally incriminated Laura Anne to me."

He had my full attention now. "Over what issues?"

"Apparently Laura Anne recently had an affair which deeply distressed Duke George when he discovered it. Gossip was that he would forgive her if she ended it. Valerie isn't sure that she did. Also Dawson revealed he'd been driving Laura Anne to London more than usual – not sure what that means. Maybe a lover's tryst?"

"Poor Duke George. So you're thinking Laura Anne may have sent the bomb, and Zachary is innocent?"

"I didn't say that. Zachary's the outsider which makes him more suspicious. We have circumstantial evidence only, but the whole thing does smell like green cheese. I'm not ready to draw a conclusion yet."

Standing taller, I raised my head to look him in the eye. "Well for one, I'm sure Zachary's innocent."

"Get me facts, then!" Blakeley pressed his fists together.

I hurried back to the rest of the family who had lingered. I followed Rosalind to the door and tapped her shoulder.

She turned around to face me.

"Might you be available tomorrow to visit privately?"

"Of course. Come by for tea." She pulled a calling card out of a tan alligator leather bag. "Here's my address. Does 10 A.M. work?

"Yes, I look forward to it."

The next day I cautiously drove the Wycham Manor spare car to Rosalind's charming English Tudor home in Knightsbridge. To my surprise Laura Anne was accommodating about her car. Most likely she'd steeled herself to put up with minor inconveniences a few more days until we were permanently gone.

I still found driving on the opposite side of the road challenging. Three roundabouts later, I was totally lost. My GPS was worthless.

I found my way back to the main road leading across the river. Traffic swarmed around me. At the crest of the hill I reached a fork in the road. I looked to my right to pull into the stream of cars then decided to take the left which was less busy. Fortunately my guess was correct. I drove a block and arrived at her property.

Rosalind's Tudor style home was tastefully decorated in tones of beige and rose. In the reception hall a gold-framed picture of a joyful Christ with His head thrown back as if about to laugh dominated the area.

Rosalind invited me to sit in an area of the living room where a tea table had been set for two. She made me feel at ease immediately. "I'm glad you suggested this. I agree it might be helpful for the two of us to visit alone. This is all such a dreadful affair. The inspector seems to trust you. What are your impressions thus far?"

"I doubt I know any more than you." I'd hoped to use this opportunity to quiz her, not vice versa. "You lived quite close to your nephew. Did you spend much time together?"

"Geographical proximity, yes, but we rarely kept up on each other's personal activities or feelings for that matter. Still I checked on him a bit. Family bonding, you know, although I think women experience it more deeply than men."

I nodded. "You're right. Often a female thing."

"I wish my nephew hadn't mocked my faith continuously. Funny how he respected my opinion about health.

We were both rather vitamin pill attics but he drew a wall when it came to spiritual talk about God. It would so comfort me to know he's in heaven." She exhaled a sad, little sigh. "One can only do so much, which is why his death is terribly tragic to me. I loved him, but hated how he teased and taunted me."

"Yes, such a horrible end," I commiserated with her. "You must have some conclusions of your own about the source of the bomb?"

"I've thought a lot about this. I do have an idea why someone would want him dead, but it's very speculative. I'm willing to tell you." Her arms shivered. "But first, tea."

Rosalind poured skillfully from a blue floral teapot into two china cups, not sloshing a drop. "Cream or sugar?

"Only one sugar lump please." Why does English etiquette require the hostess to add my cream and sugar for me, instead of letting me? Not that I mind. It's always a pleasure to be served. Long ago on a trip to London, I fell in love with afternoon tea. In my opinion, along with taxation without representation, Americans abandoned some valuable genteel customs following the revolution against England. The ritual of tea time might be worth reviving.

While serving me, Rosalind remained silent, perhaps ordering her thoughts. Fragrant mint from the teapot pleasantly filled the air. I sat on the edge of my seat waiting for her to resume talking.

Finally she said, "I remember when Duke George was a teenager. He used his allowance, a considerable sum, to order a Corvette from an American businessman over there. His dad was very controlling and insisted George sell it and purchase a more conservative car better suited to the family's image."

"How did the Duke respond?"

"George had a naughty, vicious streak. He smashed the car repeatedly into heavy metal refuse containers on the day he was ordered to sell it. He suffered no consequences for his actions. George was self-willed and destructive and totally spoiled. All this is to say I can't see him letting go of Laura Anne if she had wanted a divorce."

"Maybe Duke George saw Laura Anne as some kind of American trophy, rather than an intimate partner in marriage?"

"Perhaps." Rosalind bit into a tiny scone. "I wonder if the answer to Duke George's disaster is with Laura Anne. Not that I'm saying she's responsible, but she may know who is."

Interesting. Rosalind didn't accuse her relative of anything outright, but her remark certainly could be interpreted as believing Laura Anne was devious. "Are you implying she wanted out of her marriage?"

"Perhaps you should have that discussion with her. You might inquire regarding her personal trainer. And how exactly Duke George found out about the ongoing affair she was having with him. When he discovered their relationship, I imagine he made her stop. I've no idea how either of them responded to one another after that. This must have been very painful for my nephew."

"Although perhaps not surprising. After all, he married a divorcee. It didn't seem to bother him that he broke up Laura Anne's first marriage. Have you told the inspector about this affair?"

"Yes, I informed Inspector Blakeley privately, but he considered it immaterial."

If Rosalind had more details, she wasn't divulging any more than she had, which was plenty. Protective and loyal to her nephew. I admired this about her if it were true. Or was Rosalind another possible suspect. She professed to be a Christian, but so are some people who commit crimes under duress, because they're judgmental and unforgiving.

The reality of one's commitment to live a Christ-like life is only known to God. Rosalind could have just as easily sent the bomb if she resented her nephew deeply for his flamboyant lifestyle.

However, this personal trainer story confirmed what Valerie had told Inspector Blakeley. Had he been checked out thoroughly? Then again what about Valerie? She seemed almost obsessed with Duke George. Might she have sent the bomb out of jealousy?

CHAPTER SIXTEEN

Running late as usual, at 2:30 P.M. I hurried to meet George's contact J. Wilson whose name had been written on the note pad I'd seen in George's room. I'd briefly told him on the phone why I wanted to see him. Happily, he was agreeable. We arranged a meeting at the golf course where he spent his days. Ashley's nanny agreed to play board games and read with Jenny during my absence.

Outside, the gorgeous sky held swirls of color resembling rainbow sherbet. The intricate beauty reminded me that God is ultimately in control of all things at all times. What comfort!

Today I drove our rented Peugot which Nick had leased for his golf. With the stick shift on the left, I struggled to hug the center white line to keep from hitting curbs. UK'ers seem to be fond of these barriers to delineate their roads. To be honest, the narrow streets and frequent round-a-bouts disoriented me. I'm unaccustomed to cars parked facing me.

Finally, I arrived and hustled into the country club dining room. Fortunately Mr. Wilson hadn't arrived yet. The only staff was a mature-looking man behind the bar. He rang a bell that made a quiet tinkle, and a robust woman with dark ringlets circling her face appeared suddenly from the back like a genie. She hurried over to me.

I gave her a cordial smile. "Thanks, I'll order later, but what's your soup today?"

"Vegetable, but I'm sorry, you can't eat here, missus. You have to be a member or have one sign for you."

I was momentarily speechless. This wasn't a men's only golf club. I'd seen women on the course. The modest clubhouse with white walls devoid of décor except green, blue, and red plaid valances at the windows didn't look like an exclusive country club.

Most golfers who passed by the picture window, men and women, too, carried their own bags. Not having shoulders like Hercules, I knew I'd have rented a trolley—British word for golf handcart. I smiled, impressed with myself for knowing that word.

"It's okay," I smiled again, "I'm meeting a member." Just then a man stuck first his head, then his body through the front door. He spotted me and immediately strode over. "You must be Dr. Jennifer Trevor."

"Yes, Mr. Wilson," I said, glad to be identified in front of this woman who had made me feel unwelcome. I hate discrimination whether it's for color of skin, thickness of wallet or anything.

Wilson looked like my Uncle John, tree-like arms and way more legs than upper body.

"I'll sign for her, Mary." He gestured my way with his hand. "Join me at my usual table."

"Thanks." I followed him to a square corner table next to a bay window. Outside a misty rain had sprung up. The golfers passing by seemed quite cheery in spite of it.

"We'll get to your business over a quick lunch. I intend to get a round of golf in if this rain stays light."

"Of course. As you know, I'm here because of that horrible, err, incident George had."

"Excuse me." The plump lady interrupted us for our order. Wilson said, "Iced tea, of course. Two prawn salad sandwiches with lettuce. He looked at me and leaned closer. "That's the best thing here. Vegetable soup's good, too."

"I'll have the soup please."

"Sandwich too?" She glared at me.

"Thanks, I'm not that hungry." I spoke graciously to my rude waitress. Kindness was my modus operandi for dealing with crabby people. Perhaps ignoring her grumpiness might inspire more courtesy.

Mr. Wilson zeroed in on me. "Okay, so you want to talk about George's unfortunate demise?"

I liked how direct and matter of fact Mr. Wilson was. "Yes," I said, urging him on.

"Well, I can assure you no one from our links club was involved. George was one of the old boys. We might have killed him on the golf course though. That was a joke." He paused to grin. " Quite a good player he was, fantastic short game, did you know?"

"No, I didn't, but," I shrugged, "sadly it matters little now."

"Yep, may he be playing on the great golf course beyond."

"Can you tell me a bit about George's background, his habits, relationships. A very honorable man is being questioned as a suspect in his murder. I'm quite sure he's innocent and want to help him."

Mr. Wilson swirled the tea in his glass holding it in his right hand. "What specifically would you want to know?"

"Was George a gambler? I'm wondering if the motive for this bomb could be an unpaid debt?"

"That depends. If you call an occasional skins game on the course gambling, yes, but hardly worth killing over. Nothing more serious than that, far as I knew."

I tried another tack. "I assume Duke George's money was inherited. Is that correct?"

"Not entirely. His grandfather had squandered the family fortune years back with some bad investments. George's dad managed to gather some back. Frankly, I'm not sure of George's present status."

Interesting. I made mental notes. "Do you happen to know where he banked?"

"Now we are getting personal." Mr. Wilson eyed me up and down suspiciously. "Won't his wife tell you that if you need to know?"

"At the moment she's rather uncommunicative with me."

That raised his eyebrows. "I never did like that woman much. Nice enough looks, but not much else going for her in my opinion. She's one I'd suspect if I were you."

"Thanks for being honest with your opinion."

"Sure, honesty is how I operate. Nothing comes back to bite you later that way."

I smiled my agreement.

While we talked, Wilson devoured his sandwiches and slurped his iced tea through a straw. Finally he leaned back and studied me, maybe deciding how much info he was willing to share. I must have passed his test because next he said, "Duke George probably used one of the Barclays Bank branches. Most everybody does. Most of us do business with accountants at Biddle in downtown London if that helps you any."

"Thanks, Mr. Wilson. It does."

"Call me John."

"Please contact me, John, if anything else comes to mind." I pulled out a card and underlined my phone number before I handed it to him.

"Sure, but you might want to talk to my brother James. I can give you his number. He's been on holiday but due back soon. He and Duke George were closer than me and him."

I felt my jaw drop. "There are two J. Wilsons, then?"

He looked at me as if I were retarded. "Obviously. I'm a bachelor. James lost his wife a couple years ago. She had polio as a child and was never really well. He'd know most about explosives because he worked munitions during the war. We use the same cell number."

I determined to follow up with the other "J" James Wilson immediately.

Another reminder for me to never assume anything.

Once inside my car, I immediately reached the other J. Wilson. Fortunately, when I explained the circumstances, he was receptive to seeing me as soon as possible. We agreed to connect when he returned the next day.

On my way back to the castle, clouds covered every inch of sky creating a sense of gloom everywhere. I wish weather didn't affect me emotionally, but it does.

A short walk with Nick depressed me further. Mist hung over the facade of the castle like a black veil over a mourner's face.

When we returned to our bedroom, my romantic husband said, "Jenny is occupied with the nanny. I know just what you need." He began to unbutton my blouse.

Nick was always eager to perk me up with physical intimacy.

Afterwards, I smiled up at him as he rolled off my body. "As usual, you had a great idea."

From my vantage point stretched out on the bed, I stared at the ceiling about twenty feet above me. Nick, sitting next to me, opened his Priority Manager to review notes. I had told him during our stroll about my meeting with J. Wilson and my intention to follow up with his brother.

I could not keep the lament out of my tone. "All this grandeur and ugliness in the same place, Nick. Family tragedy and marital deceit are horrid. They make people act abominably. Any subterfuge makes me angry! It's so destructive."

Nick murmured his agreement. "What can I say to make you feel better?"

"Nothing. Just listen to me rant a bit." I laughed to break the solemn mood.

He laid his book on his stomach shaping it into a peaked roof.

"Poor George may have had no relational expectations from his marriage other than a desire to flaunt a beautiful duchess. On the other hand, Laura Anne may have coveted a title. That could have been a huge disappointment for her. She may have discovered it isn't always easy to be accepted when you marry into a position of prestige." The waitress's scorn from earlier today still rankled me.

"Righto. Laura Anne would be perceived as the woman from the States, perhaps not as highly honored as she'd hoped. Plenty of motive for dissatisfaction there." Nick closed his notebook and gazed at me. "Laura Anne's behavior doesn't make sense. Ashley is an adorable child. Why would Laura Anne be willing to give her up? I know you never could do that to one of our children."

"You're right. That's why in the back of my mind I fear she'll never go through with her offer to give up sweet Ashley. Still, it's hard to believe a woman would commit a murder to implicate her ex for which she'd surely be investigated."

"Why not? She's a duchess, George a duke," Nick said. "She'd be given every consideration in an English court by the law, although not from Blakeley. In spousal murder cases, naturally husbands and wives and ex's are always first suspects, until proved innocent by a sound alibi."

"In this bomb situation, nobody in the family needed an alibi."

"That's the beauty of absentee murder by mail. The killer is nowhere around when the act occurs," Nick added.

"I wonder just how much Laura Anne stands to inherit from his dukedom once the total estate is settled. I'd love to get those answers from her lawyer." I sighed.

"I understand Duke George owned other land in London too. Nice to know how much property he had and what's it worth." Nick grimaced. "Richard surely won't give out information without Laura Anne authorizing our receiving it."

"At this point all the motivation points to Laura Anne or her boyfriend sending the bomb at the exact time we're here to point to Zachary, of course, quite clever. An intricate set-up waiting for us to arrive. Now she's managed to delay or sabotage everything regarding his taking custody."

Nick stood and began to pace. "She won't get away with it. If that's true, she's quite diabolical. All the reason to be very careful, precious wife."

CHAPTER SEVENTEEN

Later that afternoon I was relieved to see Zachary come bounding into the castle dining room.

I immediately requested tea be served in the garden so we could have privacy. The crisp, fragrant air made life feel somewhat normal, if only briefly.

Zachary slunk into a chair. "They let me go pending further investigation because of lack of evidence. I'll feel better when we know what's happened. Any luck with your investigation?"

"I wish we had concrete news, but no substantial information regarding the culprit. Zachary, I can only imagine how upsetting this is for you. I want to reassure you, of course, Nick and I know you're not responsible for the bomb. But have you been completely forthright with us about all your communication with Laura Anne?"

For some reason I had a hunch that he hadn't. I disliked thinking that. Fact was, I barely knew Zachary. I'd trusted him even though our relationship was very fresh. In my blunt, but kind, fashion I pinned him down further. "Zachary, seriously, have you told us everything? Is there anything else that might be helpful to know?"

He shifted his eyes to the tabletop, then looked away. Not a good sign. "Why would I hold back?"

"You tell me, but I wouldn't appreciate finding out you haven't been completely honest."

I stood to leave but paused at the door and looked back.

I couldn't pinpoint why, but I still sensed he was withholding something.

He stared at me, thoughtfully. Mulling over my words?

"Zachary, remember I need to go back Monday whatever happens. I'm sorry, but I have other clients waiting on me."

His eyes took on a pleading look. "I'll pay you more, double my original offer, just wait this out with me. It may be only a few more days until Laura Anne's ready to let Ashley go. After all she's had quite a shock. Once all this settles down, I think she'll be reasonable again."

Since he was being overly generous with his financial offer, something else suddenly occurred to me. I asked point-blank. "Zachary, were you intending to pay additional money for the transfer of Ashley's custody to you beyond the agreement Nick drew up for you?"

"Just picking up a few of Laura Anne's outstanding bills, like Ashley's unpaid school tuition and a small additional settlement."

"You didn't see fit to mention this to Nick or me?"

"No," he said sheepishly lowering his head.

"I asked you not to keep anything back."

"I was afraid you wouldn't understand. It's an additional lump sum payout I can easily afford."

He named the figure. I gasped.

"Money isn't important to me, Jennifer. According to Laura Anne, George was a tightwad, even though he's loaded. I get it. Some men can't bear to part with money. Or maybe she's still a spendthrift and needs the funds. I honestly don't care."

"Regardless, that changes motivation. This entire transaction should have been in the open."

Zachary stiffened. "No way! Like someday my daughter needs to know she was bought? I think not."

"At least, this tells me Laura Anne is serious about the change of custody. She must desperately want or need that money."

"I'm sorry."

I folded my arms tightly across my chest. "Zachary, I don't appreciate it when clients don't level with me, although it does happen. I have a professional reputation to protect. I've accused Laura Anne about devious intentions and playing you."

"Try to understand. I was scared, Jennifer, that you and Nick would insist I negotiate her down because the price is so high. You know how temperamental Laura

Anne is. I couldn't risk her backing out. I worked the deal through George's personal secretary Gabrielle."

I glared at him but sensed my anger decrease when I looked into the hopeful father's pathetic eyes.

"Please don't quit on me." His voice took on a begging tone again.

"Okay, Zachary, We're here, but only a little longer."

My one little word, 'okay', and he looked like the Washington Monument had been lifted off his back.

"I hope to see this through to its conclusion. I pray it's the one we both want."

When I left Zachary, I rubbed my forehead to relieve the tightness, like someone had stretched a band around it. Rather than ask Laura Anne, I located the maid Valerie dusting the ornate breakfront in one of the dining rooms. "Valerie, I'd appreciate it if you'd do me a favor please. May I have the contact info for the secretary who handles the Duke's paperwork, address and phone number, please?"

"You'll be meaning Gabrielle Trent. Give me a moment." She returned shortly, holding a small paper with Gabrielle's information.

I was sure the inspector had already questioned Gabrielle, but from what I'd seen of the inspector's tactics, perhaps Mrs. Trent's sensibilities were offended, which could have kept her from being totally forthcoming. Besides, he may have missed something.

When I called Gabrielle, her voice sounded strained. Maybe she'd been crying. "Gabrielle, I need to ask a few additional questions regarding the Duke's recent tragedy."

"Haven't you done enough damage? Zachary Taylor and the rest of you started all this."

"Gabrielle, you aren't holding us responsible?"

"Why not? Before your arrival at Wycham Castle, Duke George was alive."

"May I come over this evening to discuss this further?"

"I suppose. It's all a mess, but I'd relish giving you my opinion. Come at seven."

I hurried back to my room. Perhaps a brief nap would help. Usually twenty minutes is enough to recharge me. Too much strain these past days. I like my life to be smooth. Events should flow peacefully. That's the goal I give my clients. I had to believe that my being here was for a good purpose, even though right now peace eluded me.

Once again, I reminded myself that Nick being able to walk the fairways at St. Andrew's Old Course was worth the trip. Next to heaven this was the one thing on his bucket list.

On the positive side, I appreciated that Laura Anne had suggested Jenny be supervised by Ashley's nanny who came daily. A kind streak must exist in Laura Anne somewhere, I surmised. Knowing Jenny was well cared for had enabled me to help with the investigation.

I ruminated over how Laura Anne had initially wanted my help to discover who killed her husband. But was this her true emotion or a superficial gesture, a ploy, to distract attention from her?

I twisted and turned until finally drifting off into a light sleep.

Nick's return awakened me.

"That felt good," he said. "I needed some exercise."

I filled Nick in on my recent conversation with Zachary.

"I'm disappointed, but not surprised." His gracious comment was, "The guy is desperate. I can't blame him. I'll go talk to him."

"Great. Sweetie, after this conversation with Zachary, I want to connect with Duke George's secretary Gabrielle as soon as possible."

"No problem. Take our rental car." He fished in his pocket, then handed me the key.

Gabrielle lived a few blocks away in one of several small apartments that had been remodeled from a larger farm building. I appreciated that she was willing to see me immediately and actually appeared rather eager.

Her physical demeanor exuded anger when she opened the door. This fiftyish woman seemed far too sophisticated for a lowly secretarial position, but I admonished myself. All work had dignity. Even a clerk in a store deserves respect for working diligently.

"I'd feel a loyalty to my employer, normally," Gabrielle said. "However in this case the Duke's dead, and truth is I never did care much for his wife. Though I didn't know her well because she was always flitting off somewhere, not much of a spouse in my opinion. And I saw firsthand the bills she ran up."

"How did the Duke of Wycham respond to her behavior?"

"He paid promptly but occasionally would murmur about her extravagance. Not that he didn't have the funds or say all that much. Makes a difference he was in a position to afford her whims. No way he liked it though."

"I imagine not." Since Gabrielle was willing to talk, I pressed her further. "What about Duke George's personal habits with money? I wouldn't ask if it wasn't relevant as to why someone would kill him. I've known of many a wealthy man in hock to his neck because of horses, gambling or other vices."

"Can't say for sure if that's true. If so, the money wasn't run through the usual household accounts. No way for me to track anything else. So I'd say, not as far as I'd know."

"Had any other mail come in the last month or so that seemed to distress the Duke?"

"Nothing I noticed. All the usual business, mutual fund reports, statements from his bank, brokers. I did mostly sorting and filing papers after the Duke read and screened his mail. And routine bill-paying. The account always had adequate funds."

"Think, Gabrielle. Did any other business correspondence raise your suspicion?"

"No."

She floundered for a minute as she twisted her position on the chair. "May as well give you my conclusion I suppose. Seems to me, Laura Anne's the one who sent the bomb. Make life a lot easier for her to have him gone." To my surprise, Gabrielle started sobbing.

"I'm so sorry. Obviously, you cared for him as any loyal secretary would. Had he seemed distressed lately about anything else, perhaps more personal?"

"The inspector asked me these same questions. I know the Duke had been having doctor's appointments, but what man his age doesn't? Bothered me that his wife never seemed to notice or care much about anything the Duke did."

"Was he easy to work for?" Vague, silly question I realized as soon as I'd asked.

"My job wasn't exciting, but there was a pleasant atmosphere working at a castle for a quiet employer. I felt a distance from him, but assumed that's the kind of working relationship he preferred. I didn't intrude in any way." She drew herself to an upright posture. "At least I knew my place."

Was there someone who didn't?"

"I meant nothing by that."

Was she implying someone didn't? Like Laura Anne?

"Thanks, Gabrielle, you've been helpful."

Questions still swirled through my mind.

Was George really as distant as she said? How strong were her feelings for him? Had Gabrielle been rejected by George and plotted revenge? Did she have regrets after killing the Duke? No wonder Gabrielle would want to accuse Laura Anne.

Would Gabrielle have had a chance to steal from his funds? She was his secretary/bookkeeper. Was she worried that Duke George would find out or already had? A lady would like this kind of killing. It didn't require being present. Just wrapping a bomb, sending it and then pouf.

I hoped and prayed for her sake she was innocent.

When I returned to the castle, I decided to unwind with a stroll through the well-lit lovely park area the gardener kept natural and uncultivated. Ahead of me, forty yards or so, I saw George's brother-in-law, Richard, exit from the castle by a side door. I might not have thought it strange except for the way he twisted his head right and left looking around with quick moves.

His action of trying to avoid being seen aroused my curiosity. I decided to follow at a distance. He headed in the general direction I was walking although he was quite a ways in front of me. His brisk pace picked up.

I sidled along, keeping at least twenty yards behind. An abundance of tree cover kept me camouflaged.

Where are you going, Richard? I intend to find out.

He paused to check his rear. I quickly shoved myself against tree bark, fast enough to avoid being seen. I was far enough away and doubted Richard knew I was out here. He seemed quite focused on wherever he was going. I observed him pass through a small aperture in the stone wall surrounding the outer edge of the castle.

Another figure appeared slightly ahead of Richard, coming from the opposite direction. The approaching twilight cast a dim shadow over the scene. I strained to identify the person he was meeting; fairly certain it was a woman from the rhythm of her walk. Perching on my tip-toes, I observed the tops of their heads. I needed just a couple more inches of height to see over the wall. I checked around for a log to stand on but saw nothing.

I edged farther along until I came to a stone wall topped with an eight-inch wide ledge. I climbed up. My head rubbed against the vines and my nose bobbed in and out of them. Let there be no bugs, I said to myself. Eavesdropping has never been my forte, but look at me now. I mentally thanked the architect who gave me this walking surface. If only she or he'd made it a little wider. Sweat collected on my brow and trickled down my palms. I pressed them against the wall lightly. If I started to fall, the vines might give me the extra help I needed to regain my balance.

Jennifer, my motherly voice objected, you have three children, what are you doing up here? I reasoned that for Zachary and Ashley's sake I had to know what was going on.

If I edged closer. Possibly, I could make out their conversation. The blood pounded in my ears and the sound of my own breathing was all I could hear. Surveillance is not my specialty. In the counseling profession, we like every word and deed in the open. Every few feet a sharp-edged piece of stucco grated my fingers. I could imagine Nick's scowl. He'd understand I was being driven by concern for a child, but no way would he like it.

So intent was I on walking stealthily that I didn't notice the branch on my path. I stumbled, falling against the rough stone wall. The palms of both my hands scraped against the jagged stone. I held my breath. The couple didn't appear to hear the noise I'd made.

I watched them reach a small building, maybe the gardener's cottage, and enter one after the other. Craning my head, I could see the open window and drapes rippling inward.

Richard's meeting didn't seem to be a lover's tryst - I heard him yelling and strained to listen. How could I get closer?

I did a quick purview of my surroundings. By creeping along the stone foundation, I could remain obscure but reach a spot where the sound might be better. I risked a peek. The woman resembled—no, was Valerie.

Snatches of quick, angry words from inside the cottage floated through the air. "Why take the drugs? I told you she didn't do it... "

"I didn't want anyone to think it was him. I couldn't bear that. He was always kind to me."

Richard gestured with his arms. "Constance knows it had to be you."

I hadn't seen Richard show this much emotional energy before. He muttered something I couldn't decipher, then turned haughtily and walked away. Valerie stood stiffly like an ignored street-corner vagrant, remaining still a full minute. Obviously, Richard's anger had upset her. I thought she was going to run after him, but instead she turned the opposite way and stalked off.

What was this about? At least now I knew why the inspector didn't find any medications.

Had Valerie hidden them to protect George's reputation as a mentally stable man? Why did she care? Richard was now close to the opening in the wall and coming my way. I ran back to a ditch about ten yards away. The wind had picked up, muffling the sound of my feet pattering through the tall grass. My black jeans and olive-green turtleneck acted as natural camouflage. I had no idea how close he was. I took a flying leap into the mound of leaves. The scent of cut grass filled my nostrils. I remained perfectly still until Richard's steps sounded past me toward the castle. Far as I could tell, there'd been no change in the rhythm of his walk. I hoped that meant he hadn't seen me. I stayed in the ditch a few minutes to be sure. When I raised my head, matted leaves stuck to my cheek.

My first inclination was to scold myself. Jennifer, I can't believe you did this! I could easily imagine Nick's response later. He knows I'm obsessing with finding George's murderer and wanting to help Zachary move forward in his life with Ashley and Lydia. My familiar tight-rope. My clients' concerns become mine.

Extreme frustration flooded through me as I rose and brushed the leaves off my face and clothes. Sorting out these interpersonal dynamics at Wycham Castle was no easy task, but I was determined. I decided not to tell Nick immediately about my exploits tonight. Why distress him further. We only had twenty-four hours left.

That night I dreamt I was in a tunnel blocked by a huge beast resembling a giant Georgia bull dog. Crushed glass on the walls brushed against my body and cut my arms every time I took a step. I had to keep moving to evade the frogs trying to crawl over my body and gnaw at me. I woke up sweating. Way too vivid for me.

One word surfaced in my brain. Bomb.

When I awoke, I had a surge of longing for my own country. Enough of aristocracy and castles. Disintegrating buildings surrounded by skeletons of scaffolding dotted the English and Scottish landscape. Continuous restoration work in Europe was as common as the historical legacies of these buildings being transferred to future generations. I wanted the safety and comfort of American soil and the pleasure of my own life with its disorderly complexity, minus explosions. Bombs didn't belong in my private world. Two nights before, my family had been sleeping in part of Wycham Castle which no longer existed now.

These events were way too threatening for me.

CHAPTER EIGHTEEN

Three loud knocks sounded on our bedroom door, breaking the silence of my morning devotions and Nick's Bible reading as he sat on the chair beside me. He rose and opened to Blakeley's assistant investigator standing outside.

The gentleman abruptly informed us that an important matter required our presence in the sitting room immediately. He explained that Inspector Blakeley had arrived at 9 A.M. with not one but two bobbies, British word for policemen.

When we entered the room a few minutes later, Zachary was already seated. An annoyed look spread upon his face. "What's this all about?"

I shrugged. "I have no idea."

Laura Anne marched in haughtily, still in her robe and slippers. Obviously, she hadn't expected a 9 A.M. curtain call either.

"Why am I being summoned to sit here? I'm calling my lawyer immediately."

"Don't bother." Blakeley's expression was sour. He hadn't bothered to remove his trench coat. "He's already been invited."

The cozy effect of the floral patterns on the wide-armed stuffed chairs was lost on us. Laura Anne's sister-in-law Constance held a box of Kleenex in her lap and dabbed her eyes every few minutes.

Once everyone on Blakeley's list had arrived, he acknowledged our presence with a curt "Good morning! We're doing an extensive search of the premises this morning including staff rooms. Let's keep this simple. I can procure a warrant in case any of you refuse to let us inspect your rooms and luggage. Or this can be voluntary - a good gesture on your part, unless of course there's a trace of any incriminating evidence among your possessions."

Nick and I were silent. How incompetent that after three days, Blakely initiated a search. Had someone tipped him off that he might discover something valuable?

Valerie and Dawson stood together silently in the rear of the room. They made no objection to the search, which made me wonder if they had instigated it.

"My men are starting now. I'd appreciate it if you'd remain gathered together here until we've finished."

Laura Anne pointed at us and said indignantly, "These people are outsiders. Search their rooms. There's no reason to suspect me."

"Righto, righto," the inspector said. "Quite a feat for a bloke like me giving orders to a Duchess, but the fact is, Duchess, I am." He smirked, obviously enjoying his superior role over an aristocrat.

Laura Anne hemmed and hawed further, threatening to report Blakeley to his supervisor.

Blakeley said, "Listen lady, I don't want trouble. Just following protocol."

Laura Anne's brother-in-law lawyer arrived. "I object to your searching my sister-in-law's room. After all, she's the deceased victim's wife."

The inspector glared at Richard. "Well, since you object, best you know that I had a case like this once before and turned out to be a close member of the family, a spouse."

Richard was helpless to do anything, other than make this initial protest on behalf of Laura Anne.

The inspector jabbed his finger at the lawyer's chest and zeroed in on him sharply. "You were a frequent house guest, and I understand you were here for dinner with these people the night before George's demise. You can stick around to see what we find."

Richard ended up captive with us.

To her credit, Laura Anne settled down and acted more docile.

The Inspector smiled, displaying his nicotine-stained teeth. He headed upstairs, leaving a bobby to supervise us.

As soon as Blakeley was gone, her lawyer brother-in-law turned toward Laura Anne. "I've checked into Blakeley. Not much class, but persistent. You may have some disruption during his investigation, but if you can put up with him, hopefully, we'll find out who did this to poor George."

Laura Anne looked away and didn't answer. I hoped she cared deeply about finding the culprit, but I wondered.

Make-up bag in hand, she went directly to the mirror to finish her cosmetics and didn't say another word to any of us.

As best I could tell, we all agreed to the search voluntarily, including the staff.

The large French doors were pulled closed, shutting us inside for morning tea and toast.

An hour and a half later, Blakeley rejoined us. "We've gone through your rooms and personal items. We found a magazine article on making home-made bombs in your laptop case, Zachary."

"What?" Zachary stammered. "That's not mine. I've never seen it before."

"See!" Laura Anne yelled.

While Zachary responded, Blakeley watched Laura Anne. "I know." Another detective kept his eyes glued on Valerie and Dawson.

That had to be a plant, too obvious to be credible even to Blakeley. Zachary would have had to be totally stupid if he were the culprit. I realized Blakeley had been bluffing but was shamelessly testing Laura Anne's reaction.

The inspector held something else in his hands, a small package. He walked over to the coffee table and unwrapped it. "Have you ever seen this before?" he asked turning toward her.

"Never," Laura Anne said.

"That's strange. We found it in your room between the mattress and the spring."

"What is it?" Her eyes glazed over like two marbles. She approached and tried to poke at the objects, but the inspector restrained her hand.

"A stick of explosive and piece of wire, both of which could be used in putting together bombs. The magazine was there also. You'll need to come with us, Mrs. Wycham, for further questioning."

Richard jumped up and strode to her side. "Don't say a word, Laura Anne."

The inspector rattled off the technicalities. "I'll read you your rights. I hope your lawyer is listening up."

When he finished speaking, Zachary approached his ex-wife with a look of disgust. "Guess I should be happy I got out of our relationship easier than George."

Laura Anne slapped Zachary as hard as she could, leaving a red welt across his face. It seemed as if all the fury she felt toward the inspector had been added to the blow for extra measure.

Zachary rubbed his cheek with the palm of his hand.

Laura Anne stared at him with absolute disdain. Her eyes could have chilled a third-degree burn. Then she snapped an order to Valerie to get her jacket.

Inspector Blakeley ignored their incident.

The cook had prepared a light lunch of our choice of egg salad or cucumber and cream cheese mini sandwiches. We ate in Wycham Manor's parlor dining room without our hostess. It seemed eerie being in the castle with its proprietor dead and the duchess a virtual prisoner. I was reminded of wars of old when kings fought against earls and squires to protect their holdings.

Afterwards, Nick and I gladly retreated to our room. I told him about the conversation I heard between Richard and Valerie. I sighed deeply. "This situation is getting stranger by the day. I don't know what to think, Nick."

"What next! I've had enough." Nick groaned. "Fortunately, we'll be leaving soon."

"How I'd hoped to see this resolved first! This bomb might have been part of Laura Anne's elaborate plan to entrap Zachary and get him out of her life forever. Of course, she expected he'd be blamed."

"If you ask if I think she's capable of such behavior, I'd say yes definitely. Some women are control and power freaks. Would she? I don't know. It's rather risky for her."

Nick summarized my thoughts.

"And stupid. Why be dumb enough to leave parts of the bomb apparatus behind in her room?"

"Who ever said murderers are smart? Still the evidence Blakeley's men found plus secretary Gabrielle's comments have to make you wonder if Laura Anne did kill her husband."

I shook my head sadly. "I wish I knew more about her daily habits, like how much time she and the Duke spent together."

We were sitting side by side on the bed. "Are you angry we're here darling?"

Nick took a moment before responding. "No, coming was the right thing initially, but I do wish we weren't part of this chaos. You get us into the most bizarre situations, Jennifer, but I admit I did introduce you to Zachary in the first place.

"True." I studied the wallpaper design of yellow flower buds between four-inch periwinkle blue stripes encircling the room. I admired Laura Anne's decorating taste, although nothing else.

With gentle fingers, I tugged Nick's head close to mine and kissed him on the lips.

He smiled. "At least we're together," he said. "And I've had lots of chances to play golf, which I'm going to do now unless you need me. It's my favorite leisure activity second only to making love to you. What are your plans for the afternoon?"

"Have a private conversation with someone who may be able to provide helpful information about Laura Anne's recent activities - her chauffeur Dawson. I'm going to track him down and visit the Duke's bank also."

"Be careful."

"Absolutely. See you later, love."

CHAPTER NINETEEN

As expected I located Dawson in the garage polishing Duke George's black Rolls Royce.

It needed no wax as far as I could tell, but I knew nothing about the care of fine automobiles. He used wide flourishing arm movements like he was leading a symphony orchestra rather than waxing a car. I would have liked to put my Subaru back home into his adroit hands.

Dawson looked up at me with a surprised look when I entered. Evidently, not many people invaded his personal domain.

I chose to warm him up with general conversation. "This is a spectacular castle. When was it constructed?"

He lit up. Obviously, I'd picked a topic dear to Dawson. "Wycham Castle was built in 1385 under Royal License from King Richard II to defend the surrounding countryside from any invading army. The French had inflicted terrible attacks on England in the early part of the 14th century, and Richard wanted fortresses throughout England.

"Come outside. I'll show you something interesting." He pointed to the northeast corner of the garage.

I eagerly followed him into the afternoon sunshine which warmed my hands pleasantly. "What are those imposing structures?"

"Stone drum towers. Identical ones protect each corner." Dawson droned on. "The duke arranged for the castle to be used as a filming location on several occasions." I could tell by the way Dawson sniffed, that wasn't to his liking. He rattled off the names of three foreign films I'd never heard of.

"If you climb the stone spiral staircase behind the garage, you'll see the upper gardens. You can enjoy the views from the battlements, but be careful, it's steep. That stone on the outdoor fireplace is worth seeing. I'll come with to keep you steady."

I shivered. Suddenly, I didn't feel comfortable having him walk behind me.

"Very nice, Dawson, maybe another time. Right now, will you please drive me to London? I'd like you to take me to Barrens & Biddle. I assume you know where that is? On the way I'd like to ask a few questions about what's been happening at the castle, if you don't mind."

"Sure, but why? Inspector Blakeley already grilled me."

"If there's anything else you can tell me that will help your deceased employer, I expect you'd like to help him."

"Don't know how."

"I'll sit in the front seat to make conversation easier."

He put on his hat and we headed out.

"For starters," I resumed, "this last month, tell me about the Duke's wife's activities. I mean where did you typically drive her?"

"She made frequent trips to London."

"More than usual?"

"Well, come to think of it, yes she did, by far."

"Exactly where did you take Laura Anne on these London outings?"

"Mostly I'd drop her off at a square. It wasn't in the best neighborhood. Kinda surprised me. Musta been part of her charity work. I took the nanny there several times too, not sure why. A poor area, lots of homeless, once I saw the nanny walking with a young girl."

He identified the area in London, and added, "I didn't like hanging around there."

"How long would she stay?"

"She'd have me pick her up one, maybe two, hours later."

"What did you do in the meantime?"

"My normal stuff. Drive around, read, listen to the radio."

"Do you have any idea who this girl might've been?"

"Maybe a friend of Ashley's? Nobody I saw close up."

"Thank you, Dawson. You're being very helpful."

"I hope so. Missus has always done right by me. I don't wanna lose both employers and have to give up this job. Taking care of these vehicles, well they are sort of like babies to me. I'd miss them."

"I understand. I'll do everything I can to assure that you remain in your position."

"Of course, ma'am, with the Duchess in custody, no problem using the car."

The London traffic was brisk but manageable. From the front seat, I absorbed the pleasant energy of the city. Everyone moved about with an aura of great purpose as if intent on accomplishing some mighty deed. I felt energized as well.

I arrived at Barrens & Biddle at two o'clock. One the way in I prayed for God to give me favor. The manager in the reception area stared at me indifferently as I made my request to speak with the accountant in charge of Zachary Taylor's custody funds distribution. "I represent Mr. Taylor." I spoke boldly and was directed to the intake secretary at a huge mahogany desk.

I approached slowly, preparing my words. Time to begin my spiel and hope for the best. "I'm assisting Inspector Blakeley in the investigation of the recent bombing at Wycham Manor." My voice came out louder than I intended. The woman, about forty-years-old, had big cheekbones reminding me of a horse's jowls.

She looked me over with a discerning eye. Then, even though I didn't have an appointment, she shuffled some papers and led me down a corridor of offices with open doors. She stopped outside the third one. "Mr. Yonder can help you." She turned and left. This had to be the favor of God.

The accountant, Mr. Yonder, threw aside business aplomb the second the secretary left. "Sit down please. Nasty affair. I was incredibly shocked." The fellow in the office across the hall eyed us curiously and leaned his neck closer.

Mr. Yonder shut the door. After some chit-chat, I brought up my involvement regarding the bombing.

"Then you probably know investigators already requested George Wycham's last year's taxes and bank statements for three months."

"Yes. I'm here because I wish they'd gone back further and looked deeper." I considered that a tidy way to put it without offending the inspector or outright asking Mr. Yonder to violate any confidences. "If there's anything that would raise an eyebrow, it would be helpful to know.... "

Mr. Yonder swiveled slightly in his desk chair before responding. "Of course, you're aware I can't reveal any personal financial information to you."

"Absolutely. In my profession I understand confidentiality, but, also in my field, murder opens that issue up to re-evaluation. I'll leave it at that. Please let me or Inspector Blakeley know if, after a further look, you come across anything irregular that you may have missed earlier."

I handed him a piece of paper with my address at Wycham Manor and cell phone number before hurrying out.

CHAPTER TWENTY

I'd arranged for Dawson to return to pick me up in an hour. Since I had twenty minutes to wait, I crossed the street, wandered down half a block and found a tea shop tucked next to a pub. I'd hardly sat beside the linen covered table when the accountant I'd seen across the hall at Barrens & Biddle came in. The bell on the wooden door tinkled behind him. He had to have followed me to arrive so quickly.

"Excuse me." He introduced himself as Robbie Dickson. "You were just at the office across from mine. May I have a word with you?"

Before I could answer, this mouse-faced man with the height of a broadsword sidled onto the chair across from me.

"You said you're investigating the circumstances regarding George Wycham's death?"

"Yes." He had my full attention now.

"I didn't want to discuss this in the office where I might be overheard, but I have a theory about the bombing." He held his breath melodramatically.

"You do?" I'd listen to any plausible idea.

"I need to be cautious. This is just between us." He looked around to see if anyone nearby was listening. Some incognito. Plus I knew where he worked. He was protecting his anonymity?

"I understand."

"First, I want fifty pounds."

I'd underestimated this disloyal opportunist. Following my gut reaction, I made a quick decision and put twenty on the table beside the salt and pepper shakers. "That's all I have on me."

Apparently satisfied, he grabbed it and leaned closer. "The Duke of Wycham's wife sent the bomb."

"You have proof of this?" Much as I didn't like Laura Anne, it was still hard to think of her as a killer.

The skinny accountant pushed his gold wire-framed glasses back on his nose. I disliked gossip, but there might be a lead here.

"I happen to know she was having an affair."

"With whom?"

He shook his head, "That I don't know."

It was hard to keep the sarcasm out of my voice. "Then how can you be sure?"

"There's no doubt."

I needed to be frank with him. "Maybe not for you, but I have plenty. Laura Anne had a nice living situation with George. For someone who obviously enjoyed material comforts, it's hard to picture her wanting out of her marriage."

He drew himself up taller on his seat. "I saw her in Soho with another child. She must have a lover and another family hidden."

"That's a big assumption. It might have been a relative or a friend's child."

"No way. I saw her sneaking around. And why would she do that if she wasn't trying to hide something?" His pale features brightened with each word.

"How old was the child? Boy or girl?"

"Hard to say, and couldn't swear to sex, what with the kid's wearing a cap and hair maybe tucked up."

I found it difficult in my wildest imagination to picture Laura Anne sneaking anywhere. "Did you follow her?" I wouldn't put it past him.

The accountant looked like I'd struck him with a scabbard.

"Of course not."

"Do you have proof, a picture, another witness?"

"No," he said reluctantly. "But what I'm telling you is true."

"Maybe you mistook another woman for Laura Anne."

"No way!" He tapped his fist on the table. "I read the society news in the paper. I know her picture too well to make a mistake. Check it out. You'll find I'm right."

I inhaled deeply. Something didn't sound right about this.

"How long have you handled the Duke's accounts?"

"Primarily his brother Richard does, but I recommended the tech stocks in his portfolio. That's my area of expertise." He puffed out his chest.

"How have they done?"

"Not well. He sold them too quickly. The whole market was volatile, but I knew it would come back. I told him to wait, but he insisted on selling. The Duke should have held out. He'd had a run of poor judgment of late. Too impatient."

Was this man trying to cover up for his incompetency in managing George's business affairs? Some people are willing to implicate someone else if it keeps them out of scrutiny.

"Did Mrs. Wycham know about his financial losses?" I wondered if she found someone else who could offer her more security. Certainly not the athletic trainer.

"Can't say I know that."

"Are you able to back up what you're saying with copies of the Duke's financial records?" I felt uncomfortable asking, but I needed facts.

Drops of moisture appeared like a magician's trick on Robbie's brow. He jerked his head back.

"I'm not copying anything, I'm just telling you what I think. The wife did it, and she's getting away with it, just like my wife did when she left me after cleaning out all our accounts. Lucky Duke George died before Laura Anne got her hands on his entire estate."

Now I understood Robbie's wagging tongue. A victim of adultery becomes a champion to protect others. C'est le vie! A French saying, and here I was in England. Frankly, at the moment, American soil seemed most attractive of all.

"If you feel this strongly, why didn't you inform the inspector?"

"I'm telling you, I can't risk my job, and you mustn't say who gave you this information. If my company knew I was talking about somebody's financials..." Robbie stood. "I gotta go."

I imagined the absurdity of ringing Inspector Blakeley with this hearsay. He'd be furious.

Still the information was puzzling. Did Laura Anne have another child born before her marriage to Zachary?

The chauffeur picked me up promptly at our meeting place, polite, and reliable, which I appreciated.

I slid across the leather seat into the air-conditioned car. Perhaps Dawson could be a source of even more information if I pumped him.

"Dawson, I'm curious about what you told me earlier about Laura Anne being in an unsavory area in

London with a young girl. Can you give me more details about that."

"Why?"

"I'm not sure, but it may be very important."

"Let me think a minute." He paused while he made a turn. "Well, Laura Anne was walking down the street eating ice cream with a young girl one time. At first, I thought it was Ashley, but when she came closer, I saw I was wrong. I kinda wondered about it."

"Anything else that you recall?"

"I saw the nanny once with a young girl who looked like Ashley coming out of a clothing store with a lot of boxes. She didn't have the boxes when she got back in this car. And the girl had disappeared. So it couldn't have been Ashley."

"Are there any other young relatives of Duke George or Anna Marie living in the castle or nearby?"

"No kids if that's what you mean. His dowager aunt lives on the top floor. She went into total seclusion after her husband's death ten years ago. Takes her meals in her quarters, which she rarely leaves."

"What about George's parents?"

"His father passed away when George was around eight from what I've heard, mother soon after. You met his sister and brother-in-law and his aunt, Mrs. Rosalind Morill. Only other kin is Aunt Josephine. Sometimes I drive her to doctor's appointments."

"Why wasn't Aunt Josephine at the family dinner?"

"As I said, she rarely leaves her quarters."

"When we get back please find Josephine Morrill's contact info on your phone and send me her number."

How had I missed this potentially valuable witness who never left the castle and might have observed something suspicious from her vantage point on the top floor?

CHAPTER TWENTY ONE

I called Josephine immediately.

"Forgive me for intruding in your grief, Ms. Morill, but frankly I'm rather desperate. My husband's friend has been accused of murdering your nephew, George Wycham. We absolutely can't believe he's responsible. I'm trying to discover who might have had enmity toward your nephew and could be the culprit. May I meet with you to discuss this?"

Her tone was icy, but still she offered me an invitation. That's all I cared about.

Josephine lived in a grace-and-favor type apartment on the third floor of the castle. I found my way through the maze of corridors to her rooms.

Although wheelchair bound, Aunt Josephine opened the door herself. My immediate impression was of a gigantic Rorschach ink blot because she was dressed totally in black.

"Follow me," she ordered in a domineering fashion and rolled off down the hall.

I inhaled a slight, but not unpleasant, mustiness from doilies draped on tables and wool blankets thrown on chairs. Her suite was charming if you appreciated genuine Eastlake antiques as I did.

Josephine motioned for me to sit, then started right in. "I'm in mourning. Poor George, what a shock."

I wondered if he was always considered "poor" George but chose not to start with that.

"You have quite a view from up here. Did you see anything suspicious on the day of the horrible incident?"

"You mean the day the bomb exploded? Might as well say it and not beat around the bush. And the answer is no!"

"Is there anything you can tell me about George that might give me a lead regarding the sender of the bomb?"

"How I wish. I've been thinking back. George wasn't calm like his father not even as a wee baby. Growing up he was a rambunctious one. Who knows what kind of trouble he got himself into or who with!" She shook her head as if in disgust.

I adjusted my position on the stiff-backed chair I sat on before commenting. "Interesting, but I'm looking into his recent activities."

Josephine appeared to be bright, and I didn't want to offend her, but our time was limited.

"I have no knowledge of his current personal affairs. George kept himself rather isolated. His mother never could cope with George and his brother Richard. They were left to themselves when they weren't at boarding school, and that pattern continued into George's adulthood. I thought it remarkable that he married a woman who seemed to have the same inability to manage a child."

"What made you think that?"

"Shipped the girl off right away when she got sassy."

I filed that for future thought, Ashley didn't seem like a snippety child to me.

Josephine continued, "If they'd let me, I could have straightened her out. I even offered, but George's wife wasn't interested in my opinion or anyone else's for that matter."

"Sounds like you didn't get on well with Laura Anne?"

Josephine either didn't hear me or ignored my question. "I never had children. I would have liked to raise my own."

"I'm sorry." I truly felt pity for her invalid state.

"God's will most likely. That's what Rosalind would say. Anyway, He allowed it. Something like that she always pontificates. My sister Rosalind's the crazy one since she started her religious nonsense. I seldom see her now."

"She doesn't visit?" I'm sure my surprise was evident. Rosalind seemed like such a caring woman.

"I refuse to let her. She prattles on about that savior of hers. If her God is so great, why am I in a wheelchair from a drunk driver's stupidity?"

"I am sorry. This isn't a perfect world. I imagine Rosalind gave you a similar answer. God gives people a free will, and terrible things can happen when evil choices are made."

Josephine sniffed loudly. "Some comfort that is."

"May I ask you a few questions about your family history?"

"You certainly are curious."

Since she didn't refuse outright, I continued. "I was wondering what happened to George's dad?"

"Died in a hunting accident." Josephine settled back in her chair. "Quite tragic."

"I'm sorry to hear that. Is there any family enmity that might have led someone to want to murder your nephew?"

"Our family was typically dysfunctional, if that's what you're asking. Anyone is capable of murder I think. Even Laura Anne, don't you agree? "

"Not everyone, no, I don't accept that. I do believe thought processes can become overactive and border on paranoid in people who have delusions of inferiority or grandeur.

"Come to think of it, one recent incident caused some hullabaloo. Laura Anne fired her sister-in-law Constance as her secretary. I believe it was a question of breaking her confidences. With good reason I might add."

"How did Constance react?"

Josephine studied the air before responding, maybe deciding how much to reveal. "Ask her. What I do know is supposedly Laura Anne was unfaithful, had an affair with her athletic trainer. Didn't surprise me one bit. Constance found out and of course she told George and Rosalind. Guess there was nothing lasting between the two of them. Not that Laura Anne wasn't capable of continuing hanky panky. Maybe he just didn't measure up to her social level."

Josephine continued to chatter on about inconsequential matters. Soon her head began to nod.

"I mustn't overtire you. I'll take my leave now. Thanks for seeing me."

"You're welcome. I normally wouldn't have allowed a visitor, but I want justice for my nephew. I certainly never had it in my life. Let me know what you find out please."

I promised I would and left. I liked Josephine. "Thank you, Lord, for this information from this dear woman," I whispered to myself and prayed for her to experience the love of Jesus despite her physical limitations. She was strongly opinionated, but seemed genuinely caring. Her fondness for George beneath her blustery words was unmistakable.

Later that evening a heavy mist coated the air. For some badly needed exercise after my day of sitting, I strolled around the castle rooms wings. Walking helps me think.

Certain pieces in this mystery at Wycham Manor weren't fitting together. I'd made the second round and was approaching George's wing when I saw a shadowy figure leaving his room. Why? Had this person taken something or planted something in the Duke's quarters? I followed quietly in my tennis shoes.

Soon I drew close enough to make out clothing - khaki pants, a flat-brimmed, tweed hat saucer-style atop the head. I couldn't be sure of gender. Perhaps a woman. If so, her hair was incredibly short or long enough to flatten under the cap. The figure left the building by way of the back entrance.

Who was sneaking around Duke George's bedroom? I'd been in there two days ago, but I figured I had a good reason. Perhaps I should be grateful I didn't catch up. If the person had turned and lunged at me, I'd no plan how to protect myself. My immediate impulses are sometimes stronger than my reason.

I went back to my room and opened my journal to reread the last pages I'd written. "We need to finalize Zachary's parenthood and return to the States quickly. Nothing makes sense. Duke George is dead. Zachary is a suspect. Laura Anne is a suspect. Laura Anne has a double life? Another child? What next?"

Nick strolled in. I immediately rattled off my latest information.

"You're a very capable psychotherapist. How do you get involved in these situations? I like when you just do normal counseling from your office."

I pulled back from his hug. "Remember who got me to London! It's all your fault." I chided him jokingly and smiled. "Seriously, wherever and whenever God wants to use me, I'm available."

"I get that," Nick said. "But let's talk this through. Safety procedures are even more important now if Laura Anne killed George. What's the plan?" Nick spoke my thoughts. "If you stop snooping around, you can avoid danger."

"Right. I'll just follow a few more threads, very safely, I promise." I plopped on the desk chair in our bedroom and opened my journal to a fresh page. I titled two lists, people and their motives.

Nick sat silently on the loveseat beside me with a faraway look in his eyes. I figured he was praying for me which I deeply appreciated. Finally he said, "George had such a negative attitude and seemed to wallow in it. I feel a deep sorrow for him."

"Me too. Attitudes can be intangible and impermanent, unless, of course, one allows them to become entrenched. Rejecting faith in God was George's choice which is why he couldn't experience the joy and peace Jesus had for him."

We were interrupted by a knock on the door at 9 P.M.

I opened to Laura Anne standing stiffly and glaring.

"Nice to see you back!" I said to soften her anger. I stepped into the hall and closed the bedroom door behind me.

"This conspiracy to involve me in my husband's death is ridiculous. The inspector questioned me and let me go, but I'm still under surveillance. Can you believe I'm a prime suspect? Jennifer, you know I'm innocent. I may know who is trying to frame me. I need you to assess my sister-in-law for me. Her behavior recently has been bizarre. She's always been a bit eccentric, but lately is unbearable. I actually wonder if she planted those items in my room."

"Why would she do that?"

"Constance has these, well, tantrums. I had to ask her not to continue handling my correspondence, and she went bonkers. I think she needs to be on medication. I had wanted to give her a work position to justify the allowance she and her husband receive. But she's disloyal, made up lies about me."

I listened wide-eyed. "I'm sorry. That had to be very distressing!" Even as I said the words, I wondered about the accuracy of Laura Anne's statements coupled with what I'd just learned from Josephine. Could Constance have precipitated this tragedy? It occurred to me that Duke George's tight hold on finances must have frustrated Laura Anne. She probably had high monetary expectations. I chose my words carefully, wanting to be kind. "Please don't misunderstand my intention which is to be supportive, Laura Anne, but it's best I not get involved in a situation between Constance and you."

"The woman's out-of-control. I'm not being paranoid. Ever since I arrived, she's been jealous of me but refuses to admit it. I'm certain she thinks of me as an enemy." Laura Anne muttered more words under her breath which I couldn't make out. Then she said testily, "I'm telling you Constance shouldn't be allowed here any longer."

I didn't want to make Laura Anne an enemy, but I couldn't allow her to pull me into this relationship. "Many of us have relatives we'd like to get rid of for one reason or another." I chuckled to lighten the mood.

Laura Anne crossed her arms in front of her. "I tell you I think Constance hates me. I want her gone."

I didn't answer but began to wonder if her sister-in-law was in danger from her. After all, Laura Anne's husband had just been murdered and she was a suspect. It seemed as if Laura Anne read my thoughts.

"Never mind. Forget I even discussed this."

But I couldn't.

CHAPTER TWENTY-TWO

Now more than ever, I needed to question Constance. The next morning I tracked her down in the library of her apartment. She answered my ring, asked me in, then returned to the wing back chair where she'd been rifling through a stack of magazines. I sat near her on a small tete-a-tete sofa.

As we exchanged small talk, I observed that her dark brown hair was striped with competing grey streaks in various shades. It looked as if she'd stopped fighting the grey and let it have its way. Like many middle-aged women, Constance had reverted to the hairstyle probably popular during her youth, a pageboy with ends flipped up, currently not in vogue, but attractive all the same.

The clothes on her extra-large body appeared tasteful and expensive, hiding what's euphemistically called a full figure. Laura Anne and Constance couldn't have been more different in appearance and personality.

I switched topics to the point of my visit. "Constance, what are your thoughts about this shocking event at the castle?" I purposely avoided the ugly words bomb and death.

Constance leaned closer and to my surprise was quite willing to share her opinion. "I'm sad but not surprised. My brother-in-law George said to me on several occasions, 'Lighten up Constance, you're always expecting the worst. Life is to be enjoyed. You often act like you're swimming upstream through rough water.' Turns out I was right about this woman."

"What do you mean?'

She thrust her shoulders back. "Well, if you ask me, he was the one who didn't recognize the reality he lived in. I'd urged him to be less trusting when he came home with his American bride. You didn't have to be around Laura Anne long to conclude she's self-willed and greedy. The woman never did fit in. And now the worst has happened." She harrumphed.

"So you didn't get along well with her?"

"Laura Anne's life could have been happy, but she kept picking at my brother-in-law until I think even he couldn't stand it. A natural trouble-maker that woman, never content, always wanting more."

I formed a mental note of Constance versus Laura Anne from the start of the Duke's marriage.

Constance continued. "I admit my brother-in-law had a bit of a negative personality, but Laura Anne pandered to it and drove him nuts. He was paranoid about financial disaster, and she spent his money like water."

Duke George's sister Constance seemed to know a lot about the Duke's marriage. Then again, she had been Laura Anne's personal secretary at the start. She rattled on, telling me horror stories about their relationship. Was it more than she'd told the inspector?

"How did Duke George respond?"

"Well, his actions will tell you the answer to that. He changed his will and started giving even more money away during his lifetime. I gathered she didn't like that, not one bit."

"I'd heard the family has a history of altruistic giving, lots of philanthropy?"

Constance laughed. "George, yes, Laura Anne? I wish. She'd steal from an orphanage if she could get away with it."

I flinched at the venom in her tone. Strong words, nothing like a sister-in-law's love between them.

Another thought blindsided me. I cringed. If Laura Anne was George's killer, Constance could be in danger. Was she the next target?

While chatting on, Constance said not all was bad in their relationship at first. She'd traveled with Laura Anne to St. Andrew's for several Christmas shopping outings.

"How were they?"

"Fine. We went for long weekends and stayed at St. Andrew's Hotel at the Old Course. They have a wonderful spa, you know."

No, I didn't know and wouldn't be putting that on my excursion list. "Did Ashley accompany you?"

"Yes. I enjoyed her company. It was a treat because I seldom got to see her."

"By the way, do you have pictures of Ashley? I'd love to see some childhood photos."

Constance walked over to the credenza, then changed her mind and rummaged through a white secretary instead. "Somewhere in these old albums..." I noted her attractive French country furniture, totally the opposite of Laura Anne's stiff formality.

A few minutes later she handed me a picture of Ashley, Duke George, Laura Anne and Aunt Rosalind admiring a Christmas tree. I couldn't see Ashley clearly. She must have turned away when she realized her picture was about to be taken.

"Nice. Who took this?"

"One of the servants, I suppose. Why?"

"Just wondered if it was another family member. When I counsel families I often study their dynamics through group pictures, which can reveal lots about relationships."

"Really, how's that?"

"By the proximity of where people stand. It's a technique I use to study children's creative family drawings.

Do they place themselves near parents? Is the family cozily sitting in a room doing individual activities or joint? It's best to see several pictures, of course, but even one can sometimes give an impression."

"What kind of relationship is Ashley displaying here?"

I chose not to answer directly but I got a vivid concept of a child who didn't feel close to the other members of her family.

Constance didn't wait for my reply. She opened another drawer. "Here's one of her drawings from when she was eight. She sent it to me. I like to think from fondness, but I suppose it was a school assignment to reach out to a relative. I've never been close to Ashley. She guards her feelings. I used to send her cards occasionally, but she rarely acknowledged them. Didn't seem as if they meant anything so I stopped."

I studied the colored picture Constance handed me, obviously one that Laura Anne had missed, or maybe she thought Ashley was too young when she drew the picture for it to matter. A tiny figure stood at the corner of the page. It had to be Ashley. Her figure was the smallest. A male stick figure was in a black crayoned house. A woman, maybe her mother, stood on the other side next to a bush resembling a green ball dotted with cotton.

Seeing the drawing made me sad. I helped Constance put the pictures away. As I was about to leave, she dropped a figurative bombshell on me.

"You might be interested to know a sniper shot at, but fortunately missed, killing my brother-in-law George on his morning walk several weeks ago. A friendly Collie dog, Duke George's favorite breed, had approached him, and he spent several minutes petting the dog and visiting with the owner. That delayed him considerably which changed his normal arrival time at the corner by several minutes where a sniper waited. Duke George was unhurt and managed to quickly get a call off for help."

Shocked, I shook my head, as if in disbelief. "I had no idea this happened. Did the authorities catch the shooter?"

"No. Whoever it was dropped the weapon and left it behind. It couldn't be traced and had no prints. The sniper evidently was wise enough to wear gloves. He or she took off running toward town and got lost in the traffic."

"How frightening for Duke George."

"Yes, his life may have been saved by that last minute encounter with the Collie. From then on when the Duke left the castle a bodyguard accompanied him."

Sick sensations roiled in my gut. Why hadn't the inspector thought to mention that there had been an attack on Duke George's life the previous month? Because it was a different type of assault? A gunman? Ideas bounced crazily in my brain. Who? A family member? Or had someone ordered and paid a professional sniper?

Surely the inspector had all the facts, but probably hadn't thought it necessary to tell me! I tamped down my annoyance.

Sometimes I dislike being a trained counselor who looks beyond the obvious and questions individual motives and behavior. Was this a genuine attack or had Duke George set up the entire incident as a fake event to elicit sympathy. If so why? Or was he trying to divert attention from another plan yet to come? Could he have been that methodical about deception?

The Duke's philosophy of life opened the door to speculation. What evil the human mind can descend to without God! If only Aunt Rosalind or a friend, anyone had been able to penetrate Duke George's arrogance with truth.

In situations like this, I cling to a modicum of hope. I prayed that at the last second before death Duke George regretted his past rejection of faith and called out to God who was perpetually near and ready to rescue a lost sheep.

I left Constance feeling intense stress. I'd learned more facts I expected from my visit with her. The mystery pieces were starting to hang together in a disturbing fashion, but still I couldn't quite put them all together. Perhaps because I didn't want to admit where this was heading.

When I returned to our suite in the castle, Jenny met me at the door. I reveled in her big hug. She'd been playing with Ashley's huge doll collection. At least Laura

Anne indulged her daughter materially if not always emotionally.

"Jenny, I hope you're not sorry that I've brought you on this trip."

"Of course not. I loved meeting Ashley. It's okay, Mom. I know helping people is what you do. It's not your fault that it's taking longer than you thought."

I smoothed her hair with my hands. "Right, Honey, these circumstances are unusual. Mommy typically helps people solve personal problems fairly easily. This has been a very complicated situation."

"Does Ashley have personal problems?" Jenny asked matter-of-factly. "Can kids have serious problems?"

"Sometimes, sweetheart.

"Will I, Mom?"

I hugged her more tightly. "I pray and think not. Most of the time problems occur in children who don't feel loved. If they learn early about God's love for them, even sad feelings of missing parents' love rarely causes deep hurt."

"Well, I'm glad you and Daddy love each other and all us kids and take good care of us." Jenny nestled her head against my shoulder.

"We sure try, honey."

"Always." Nick added, as he walked into the room and caught the tail end of our conversation. He pulled us into a group hug.

I pressed in tightly welcoming this serene moment with my husband and daughter. The entire affair over Ashley's custody and Duke George's death had me unsettled. If only I weren't so sensitive. I've wished that a thousand times. Nick says my emotions are what make me an excellent counselor. He's probably right. Although I can't stop my compassionate feelings from coming, I mustn't let them overpower me!

Pulling away from our hug, I said, "We need to quickly resolve the mystery of Duke George's death, get Ashley home to begin her new life with Zachary and return to our normality. Enough of this."

Nick grinned. "I vote for that."

CHAPTER TWENTY-THREE

I cradled the phone against my ear while rearranging the pens on the desk in front of me for the third time. "Inspector Blakely, please." I stood alone in the reception area foyer. Blakeley was going to be furious. He wasn't too thrilled with my input, lukewarm at best. Now, I was going to interfere more. I'd risk his displeasure as long as he would follow through with my suggestion. I wouldn't ask him why he'd never told me about the sniper attack on the Duke. That was his prerogative and perhaps he hadn't thought it relevant to the current issue. Why not I couldn't imagine.

"Inspector, it's just a hunch, but if you haven't already done so, I feel it's important to get a current report on Duke George's physical health. I know that may sound weird." I knew better than to push too hard. Blakeley's grudging respect for me as a detective had limits.

"Quite right. How would his health affect opening a mail bomb?"

I braced myself. At least he hadn't sworn, but here's where the inspector might go ballistic. I'd gone this far, so I spit out my theory. "What if he had some fatal illness that made him do something drastic to himself?"

I gulped. I had no evidence for this statement, just a gut feeling that seemed to make sense. I blurted out, "His aunt said he was a vitamin pill addict and very health conscious. Some people can't handle sickness well."

"So? You Americans watch too much drama."

I refrained from saying I hardly ever watch TV. "What harm can it do to contact his doctor?"

"I already have." Blunt as usual, the inspector blurted out his findings. "George Wycham took Prozac. He's been on one anti-depressant after another for a year."

Of course I couldn't tell the inspector that I already knew. Instead I asked innocently, "Who prescribed it?"

"His MD."

"Better if it had been a psychiatrist. There would be a more detailed evaluation and records." Deep in thought, I spoke absentmindedly into the phone. "If only we knew who or what was causing his anxiety and/or depression." I stared at the swirling pattern embedded in the marble tile around the fireplace in my room. Of course, distress could come from a thousand directions, some of them real only in a person's head.

"Perhaps worrying over keeping his beautiful, young wife happy. I doubt it was money problems. But the fact is there's more."

I focused on Blakeley's voice again. He was dragging words out slowly as if he didn't want to say them.

"The Duke's been seeing an oncologist for a slow-growing terminal cancer of the blood. Poor bloke. But it was being managed by oral chemotherapy. No wonder he needed an anti-depressant. As for his financial affairs which you're going to ask me about next, as I told you they were a cause for happiness not concern. What Duke living in a castle wouldn't be content?"

I'd counseled too many wealthy clients to think that ribbons of happiness were attached to financial security, but cancer! Sadness for Duke George overwhelmed me. I bit my tongue. "This might explain everything. What if he were despairing over his cancer diagnosis and feared his imminent death. Might he be tempted to commit suicide to implicate his unfaithful wife in the act?"

"You have quite an imagination. Let me be sure I'm getting this theory straight, Dr. Trevor. You're implying Duke George Wycham was crazy over thoughts of his impending death and sent the bomb to himself? And he wanted to punish his wife by setting her up as the culprit."

"I'm only speculating. Laura Anne could certainly have sent it to her husband if she wanted to be free again to remarry. I will admit I was with him two nights before he died, and he functioned quite well intellectually and physically, so obviously the cancer was presently under control."

"His wife's the one, that's what I think." Blakely's tone was adamant.

"But with all due respect, you're ignoring something. On the other hand, the Duke although intelligent and capable didn't believe in God's sovereignty over life. He may have been deeply emotionally distressed finding out his wife was having an affair. Plus his failing health could have greatly upset him, Inspector. Please give this some consideration. After all, I'm trained to evaluate people's mental state."

"I suppose your theory is a possibility."

"I admit it's based on assumptions and realize we need proof."

"Correct!" Inspector Blakely made a deep, throaty noise of displeasure. "Conclusive evidence, not just your speculating and interfering!"

I caught myself before exhibiting my annoyance with him. It was stupid to get upset over the Inspector's chameleon reaction to me. One minute I was a godsend, next I was a meddling American. A nasty thought bounced into my brain. Maybe I should comment on examining Inspector Blakeley's mental health. My tongue savored the words, but I stopped myself from speaking. Jennifer, be kind.

“Strange thing is,” Blakeley continued, “We didn’t find any anti-depressant meds in his bathroom. We checked his clothes’ pockets, too.”

Again I remembered the prescription of Prozac in his bathroom, but chose not to admit I’d been prowling around there. “Perhaps the meds were removed so we wouldn’t find them and realize how ill Duke George was, which would make us consider this path of self-harm,” I stated. “Do you agree that’s a possibility? This could be of enormous value.”

But I was talking to a dead phone.

CHAPTER TWENTY-FOUR

Lying is not my strong suit. I respect truth and don't believe in the idea of stretching it. Which is why, as I dialed Ashley's school, I was surprised that I didn't feel guilty.

A stiff grandmotherly voice answered. "Good day, Waverley Academy, Mrs. Drake speaking."

"Hello. I'm calling on behalf of Mrs. Wycham. Since the Duke's death, I'm handling some personal details for her. She wants to be sure Ashley is faring well. Will you put her on the line please?"

All true, just not in that order. While I waited, I rationalized that I'm handling details involving Laura Anne's life and I expect she wants to know how her daughter is doing.

There was a long pause. Sensing skepticism in her, I gulped. Ever since I was six and got caught in a lie, I've never been able to lie well. I think it's the memory of my mother's hair brush on my bottom to the tune of "Don't you ever deceive me, you hear!"

"Who is this?" The woman's voice asked gruffly. "Ms. Wycham knows our standard procedure. After what happened to the Duke, we certainly will not deviate. Goodbye."

I grimaced but wasn't surprised at her response.

Fortunately I am determined. I waited a few hours and tried again. Sometimes late shifts are not as carefully trained.

"This is Mrs. Wycham's representative. She wishes to speak with her daughter. It's an emergency. Please fetch Ashley."

"Yes, mum, it'll be a few minutes. We'll have to collect her from her activity."

"I'll wait on the line."

I heard clunky footsteps in the background departing and returning. Finally she said to the girl she'd fetched, "It's your mum." And to me, "Mrs. Wycham, your daughter's on."

I waited several seconds hoping the administrator would move out of earshot.

"Hello, Ashley. How are you?"

"Who's this? You're not my mum!" A cheeky, high-pitched girlish voice said nastily.

"Your mum asked me to call and check on you. You do remember me, don't you? We were in Edinburgh last Friday."

"I don't know what you're talking about. I was at a friend's in Cambridge all last weekend. Besides Mum would call me herself. Who are you? What's this about?" Ashley sounded haughty, spoiled. The phone clanged as if dropped on the desk. "Mrs. Simons!" the girl screamed. "This isn't my mum!"

Mrs. Simons grabbed the phone back and demanded, "Who is this?"

I hung up.

Anger pulsed through my veins and one all-consuming thought. Confront Laura Anne.

I almost bumped into the maid Valerie in the hall. "Where's your mistress?"

"Out. A friend of hers picked her up."

"When is she expected back?"

"I've no idea, ma'am."

"Please give her a message that I'd like to see her as soon as she returns."

The pieces began to tumble together. Laura Anne's trips to London, the homeless children, the nanny's complicity. What an ingenious plan! Who would ever expect that she could pull this off? I shuddered to think that she almost did.

I prayed. "Lord, what now?"

I strolled through the rooms at Wycham Manor with uneasiness. Any semblance of English hospitality had disappeared. My enjoyment of the environment at Wycham Castle had turned into participating in a death investigation, plus anxiety for my family in the company of these people.

For sure, I'd never open a package mailed to me with the same careless abandon.

I remembered driving by the Thames River our first night in London. Nick had explained it once was virtually a giant sewer but had been cleaned up so that fish venture downstream past Big Ben again. This whole trip smelled rotten to me. Only God could clean up this mess.

Earlier I'd received a call from James Wilson who was finally back in town. I made an arrangement to meet him for lunch to discuss his friend Duke George. I found Dawson outside watering flowers.

"May I take the spare car briefly, Dawson, for a personal errand?"

"Where to?"

I bristled at the inappropriateness of his question.

"I won't be long." I refused to tell him my destination of course. Why should I?

He hesitated. I assured him I was an excellent driver and would be cautious. After what I'd just found out, I was paranoid about trusting anyone at Wycham Manor with information.

Light rain began to patter my windshield as I pulled up to the Whispering Swan pub, a dimly lit place with about eight tables inside. I don't normally drink coffee, but tonight the familiar fragrance tempted me the second I walked in. Coffee is so "normal." And the events at

Wycham Manor were so bizarre. The bartender apparently handled food orders, too. I approached the bar to order a cup and explained I was meeting someone and would order food later.

I chose a table close to the fire to watch the golden flames and hopefully enhance my focus. Twenty minutes passed with no James Wilson. Then thirty. The rain intensified. Had his brother tipped him off causing him to avoid me now?

After two plus cups of coffee, my brain fizzed with caffeine. A hum of joshing style conversation came from the bar area. Everybody who walked in commented on the rain and the crackling lightning and thunder. The bartender and I had heard at least six weather reports thus far according to my count.

The group at the bar increased and huddled closer. Every now and then one of them glanced my way. The bartender would muffle something, and they'd turn back to their drinks.

The rain stopped briefly then picked up again with a continuing drumbeat on the roof. I thought about my childhood nights in bars, performing my ABC's at age four so my Dad could show me off. I knew I was his joy, I only wished I didn't have to talk to liquor-saturated men with foul breath.

Finally, I had to admit that I'd been stood up. My stomach growled. I wasn't leaving without food. I'd told Nick to eat without me.

I went to the bar and ordered fish and chips. The bartender took one look at my face and decided not to comment on my friend's no-show.

I'd just started eating when a big man stomped in and slapped a sloshy raincoat and wet hat on hooks by the door. He looked around with an agitated expression, then bounded toward me.

"Ah, you must be the lady I'm to meet. Sorry, miss. I was busy catching up on mail most of the morning, then took a nap, almost slept clean through to morning. My dog got scared of the storm and woke me with his barking. Had my alarm set, but musta shut it off."

I appreciated his apology. "No problem."

"May as well get a bite as long as I'm here." The tight knit group separated when James Wilson approached to place his order.

He came back with a pot of tea and a cup and saucer.

"I understand you've been on a hiking trip in the area?"

"Yes. Beautiful country this is, but desolate and dangerous, too, mind ye, every year some don't get home alive."

I shuddered. "Glad you did."

"Now what can I tell ye that will help poor Duke George."

"For starters, what was the Duke like? I only just met him and didn't get a chance to know him well."

"Nice enough chap. I'm no psychologist like you said you are so I don't know how to answer that. I can tell you what we did together. Mostly golf, an occasional dinner.

He didn't like going to London near as much as his wife. Often he'd be dining alone and invite me over."

I took a sip of my coffee. "What kind of things did he talk about?"

"Hard to say." He leaned his chair back and balanced on the rear legs. "Everything and nothing."

"Was there anything you noticed recently about George that seemed unusual? Did he appear stressed at all?"

He rubbed his full beard and thought a minute. "Not really. We talked more about me than him. He liked to hear my tales about the war. He'd never been, you know. I'm not sure why. Suppose his family kept him out somehow. He was always interested in my work with intelligence. I was an explosives expert."

"Yes, your brother told me." I zeroed in. "Why did the Duke want to know about that?"

"Actually he was into fireworks too. Always put on quite a show at the castle. He'd also read a number of intelligence books. He'd ask me what it was really like during the war. Always wanted me to recommend more reading."

"What kind of books?"

"Procedures, explosive materials we used, that sort of stuff. George was very well-read overall. A variety of interests from art to war to golf. He was always trying something new with his golf swing. Never quite got it to his satisfaction."

"This might seem to be a surprising question, but I wonder, did he seem to enjoy his family?"

Wilson bristled. “Now I don’t know about his personal life. I never asked much. And he didn’t talk about his wife either.”

“Back to the war and your conversations about explosives, you said you worked with them?”

“More than I wanted.” He elaborated on a few close escapes.

“The books that you recommended for the Duke.” I tried to keep my tone causal. “Do you recall any of the titles?”

“Sure. Espionage techniques. Bomb components. He was fascinated by the stuff. He said he had some tree stumps on his property he needed to have removed.”

Mr. Wilson mentioned three books which I jotted down in my Priority Manager.

“Thank you. You’ve been most helpful.”

“I have?” He seemed surprised. “I hope I’m not saying anything out of turn here. I just want the bloke who did this to come to justice.”

“That’s my goal as well.” I stood up.

Wilsons’ eyes flashed like hot yellow ovals as he caught my meaning. “Wait a second, you don’t think…” A groan escaped him, but he said nothing.

The English are above all loyal. How else could Winston Churchill have known he could depend on England’s response to his words, ‘We shall never surrender.’”

“I hope not, Mr. Wilson.” I exited hastily.

In my car I checked out the location and hours of the local bookstore. Time to regroup. I had a hunch there wouldn't be a totally satisfying ending to finding this truth, but maybe at least some good could be salvaged. If I didn't believe that I'd have quit searching right then. But I didn't want to leave without knowing. And we had only one day left. I called Nick before heading to the castle and arranged to pick him up.

CHAPTER TWENTY-FIVE

At 4 P.M. Nick and I were outside the Happy Bookworm bookstore skimming pictures of the volumes displayed in the shop window.

Inside we found a white-bearded elderly man and middle-aged woman. The gentleman had extremely hunched shoulders, might have been 6" stretched upright. Both welcomed us with a friendly hello. One of my favorite smells delighted my nostrils, the mustiness of old books combined with new book paper and ink. Floor to ceiling book stacks surrounded us.

"Let us know if we can help you find anything." The lady spoke softly while grabbing a feather wand to dust. The man, most likely her husband, positioned himself on a stool behind the counter and resumed reading a book. He flicked his full beard continually with the first two fingers of his left hand. With a girth so wide I doubted he could fit easily through the crowded aisles.

I disliked disturbing him or anyone for that matter who was occupied reading, even though he was the proprietor. I consider reading a near-sacred activity, but time was of the essence.

"Sir, I'm looking for these three books." I handed him the note I'd made at the pub.

"Let's see. We may have one. He circled a title. Emily, find this please." She scurried over, and he passed her the paper.

Ten minutes of hunting didn't produce any of the books we requested, but in the meantime Nick and I studied the description of each in the Books In Print conveniently out on one of the long counters.

After a few minutes, I nudged Nick. "I have another hunch."

Turning back to the proprietor I asked, "Would you be so kind as to check recent orders placed by Duke George Wycham."

"Kinda personal information, don't ya think?" the gentlemen said. "Never done that before."

I smiled and assumed my most confident, authoritative voice. "Totally not out of line in this situation. I'm assisting Inspector Blakely in an investigation regarding him." I handed him my business card as a counselor which for some reason seemed to impress him enough to hear me out. "We need to know if Duke George Wycham ordered any books on explosives. It would be a great comfort for his widow to have this information."

Did that sound like a farfetched request? Possibly, but it worked. Maybe something about bookworms causes them to be trusting.

Five minutes later I learned George Wycham had ordered two of the books on my list about explosives. I snapped a picture of the orders.

This information wouldn't have been forthcoming at Barnes and Noble in New York. I thanked God we were in England instead.

Outside the store, Nick raised his hand to give me a high five. "Jennifer you did it, I don't like what we've found, but it makes total sense."

As we walked to the parking lot, I remarked, "Nick, one thing continues to puzzle me. Why did Valerie hide George's psychiatric meds?"

Nick slipped his arm around my waist. "Maybe it was about George's will. The Duke might have informed her about his bequest. Perhaps Valerie thought Laura Anne might dispute the inheritance she and Dawson were to receive with their long-term living privileges if Laura Anne could question the Duke's mental state. But then Valerie was rather protective of him in general. It could have been an impulsive gesture Valerie regretted later."

"You're right. There certainly was no love lost between Laura Anne, Constance and Valerie. How sad the relationship webs we weave when we don't love and forgive as Jesus desires."

CHAPTER TWENTY-SIX

When we returned to Wycham Manor, Nick and I asked Zachary to join us for a private dinner served in the castle dining room. Beforehand I prayed quietly, "God give me wisdom and the right words to soften Zachary's pain."

How I hated to be the bearer of such shocking news, but Zachary had to know.

I descended the stairs, collected a cup of tea and went to sit beside Zachary and Nick.

Zachary looked up immediately. "There you are. What have you found out?"

I paused, again praying silently. "Zachary, I wish I knew an easy way to present this," I started out slowly. His eyes became wary. I explained what we'd discovered about his daughter.

"Westminster area has a large number of homeless. Londoners call them rough sleepers. That may have given

Laura Anne her subterfuge idea. Laura Anne and her nanny found a bunch of street kids living under a bridge. Sadly, lots of children are in this situation because of family poverty or abuse. The nanny made several trips and had multiple interviews before selecting a girl to pretend to be your daughter. Then Laura Anne probably met and interviewed her personally before giving the final okay."

When I finished, he looked as if he'd been gut-punched.

I added as sensitively as I could, "That would be why Laura Anne couldn't allow Ashley to come back to the castle with us. The staff would know immediately that she was an imposter.

"You're saying Ashley's not my Ashley but another girl?" The color drained from his face. He stood and turned away from me. "I need some time to process this." We watched him head outside.

When Zachary returned about half an hour later, he joined us in the living room. He plopped on the sofa and took a deep breath. "It is what it is. Have you confronted my ex-wife yet?"

"No, we thought you'd like to be present."

"You bet I would."

As if on cue, suddenly Laura Anne swaggered in wearing a nylon jogging suit in a soft shade of peach and carrying a tennis racket. She plopped it into a tall ceramic urn at the door.

"That felt good. I needed some exercise to deal with all this turmoil." Laura Anne strolled over and poured coffee from the sideboard.

"Laura Anne, we need to talk," Nick announced firmly. He strode over and closed the French doors so no one else would intrude.

"Sit down, please," Zachary demanded.

Something in his demeanor clued Laura Anne to pay attention. She took a seat at the table directly across from us and gave Zachary a bored look. "Now what? And why must you make everything sound so dramatic."

Zachary let loose with a verbal barrage. "Don't give me your coy routine. I've had enough! Where is Ashley?"

"At school of course. I'll call her right now, and you can talk with her if you like."

For a second, Zachary looked confused. "Get her on, then..." Zachary handed her his cellular phone.

"On second thought, why bother her? This isn't necessary. You'll see her soon."

"I insist." Nick's voice had an edge like steel.

"You need to understand that I don't care what the three of you want." Laura Anne pushed away his phone. "I want you to get out of here, all of you. I'm sick of this."

Zachary straightened. "I'm not leaving without a legal custody agreement that opens the door to my having a real relationship with Ashley."

Laura Anne pounded her fist on the table. "You'll never take her away from me."

I'd kept silent as long as I could. I stood up. "Zachary knows the truth, Laura Anne. You created an incredible deception. What led you to do this?" I waited to hear her twisted explanation.

As she stared at me, I watched her eyes turn black. Was she assessing if we knew the total truth?

I pressed further for an explanation to this bizarre plan. "Laura Anne, what prompted you to find the decoy who pretended to be Ashley?"

She stiffened visibly, obviously realizing now that we knew everything. Laura Anne rubbed her forehead with the back of her hands. Trying to block us out?

Finally, she said, "In London's homeless area there are plenty of waifs..."

"Yes, but why on earth would you do such a thing?" Zachary demanded.

She turned to face Zachary. "I knew you'd keep bugging me. You didn't want your daughter when she was conceived, you have no right to her now!"

Zachary exploded, "You never gave me a chance!"

Laura Anne slumped, but held her head erect.

"Who is the pretend Ashley?" I asked.

"Lizzie's a street girl."

"How did you manipulate a child to behave this way?"

"Ashley's nanny helped me train her. Lizzie was only too eager to have a chance to go to America and live with a man who would treat her like his daughter."

I rolled my eyebrows at such intricate deceit. "And you actually expected to get away with it?"

"I paid the nanny well. Plus Lizzie is bright and was desperate to have a better life, as you can imagine. I could have managed the switch nicely except for the hoopla following George's death."

I nodded. "True, you almost pulled it off." I hated to hear her speak of Duke George's death so coldly. I'd heard that tone in people who get a divorce and kill their feelings for their ex. Often, it's as if the spouse had died. Only this time George, her spouse, was dead which made it seem even worse.

"How did you get the nanny to go along with this criminal behavior?" Nick asked.

"Her job was at stake if Ashley left. And I threatened to fire her if she didn't co-operate. Offering a huge bonus helped, too." Laura Anne pushed back a strand of hair that had fallen across her face.

Zachary shook his head visibly disgusted. "And the phony Ashley, I mean... her real name you said is Lizzie."

"Yes, Lizzie. She had no last name that she remembered."

"What was her background?" Zachary appeared intent on getting the full truth now.

Laura Anne spoke so coldly that it was hard to listen to her words. "Her parents abandoned her when she was four. She's been in orphanages and foster homes ever since. That is, until she ran away from the last one, which is why she was living on the streets."

Zachary gazed silently at Laura Anne. I could only imagine his thoughts.

"Lizzie's extremely smart and sweet," I pointed out.

Zachary agreed. "You bet she is. You had no right to manipulate her emotions like this."

Laura Anne seemed eager to justify her actions. "Lizzie said she always dreamed of going to America to live. It was easy to persuade her, although I could tell she was having second thoughts about fooling you. She scared me when she disappeared for a time. Now you know everything, and it's over, stop badgering me. I did nothing criminal."

"Not so fast," I interjected.

"What do you want from me?" Fearful, Laura Anne looked from Zachary to me.

I jumped in without a second's hesitation. "Your full co-operation. A meeting between Zachary and his real daughter with complete honesty about his desire to be part of her life."

"He can't have her. Absolutely not! She's all I have left now." Laura Anne jumped up.

I thought quickly, weighing what would be best for each child. I knew what Zachary wanted. "Nick will draw up legal documents guaranteeing Zachary will speak to his daughter by phone weekly and arrange for joint custody with a month-long visit once a year. Is this acceptable, Zachary?"

Zachary stood as well and gazed into her face. "I should by all rights fight you, but I won't take Ashley away from you. You've lost enough, Laura Anne." He recited this slowly enough to give her time to comprehend. "I just want enough time with Ashley to show her what a loving father with Christian values is like and to influence her positively in that direction."

I was impressed at Zachary for showing compassion for his scheming ex-wife. I heard a strong determination in his voice, not present before.

"And I want Lizzie," Zachary announced in an insistent tone with words cutting like steel. "She's coming back to America with me and I'm adopting her as my daughter if she'll agree."

We all stared at him. Laura Anne gasped.

Nick spoke first. "That's a great plan! Your Christian principles are serving you well."

Zachary went on, "If you fight me on this, Laura Anne, I'll expose the whole sordid affair."

"No one would ever believe you!" Laura Anne stomped her foot.

"Maybe not, but the scandal mongers will have quite a time with it, won't they? And I want to give this dear disadvantaged child Lizzie, who I thought was my own daughter, a decent home in America."

"I have no problem with you having the waif. Take her! She'll be thrilled. Just so you leave Ashley in my primary custody."

I had to ask, "Did Duke George know about the deception?"

"Yes."

"What was his response?"

Laura Anne turned her face away before she answered. "He never said much about it."

"Maybe not, but I bet it distressed him to see the level of deceit you were capable of. He was already unable to trust you after your affair with the athletic trainer."

"Sad as this is," I resumed, "it makes total sense. You were doing the same thing to your daughter that George's mother had done to him when you abandoned her to boarding school. That might have seemed normal to him, although it didn't mean he liked it. Then to top it off, Laura Anne, you implicated the Duke by telling him about your plan to deceive Zachary about Ashley. He probably figured his life, what was left of it, would be miserable, because he could never have a truly loving relationship with you."

"Yes, the poor Duke finally knew what a gem he'd married." Zachary sputtered.

Nick picked up on Zachary's comment. "Duke George chose to die before you rejected him. He didn't want public scandal. And with his precarious health he knew it was just a matter of time before his death anyway."

"Duke George has paid you back rather well, hasn't he?" Zachary sounded satisfied.

"If you mean by hiding the bomb components in my room, yes." Laura Anne's voice was thick with emotion. "George could be vicious. He certainly had a flair for the melodramatic. I can't say I'm deeply sad over his death."

"Oh, but you will be," Nick spoke again. "The final stipulations of the will have been released. It's even in the newspaper since it impacts the public. You'll be leaving the castle soon. Duke George arranged for it to be turned over to the National Registry of Historic Sites upon his death. The entire property will be a museum once the restoration project is complete. Your income won't be comfortable, but it will be minimally adequate. You may need to get a job."

"What about Ashley's financial welfare?" Laura Anne snapped back. "You wanted to father her and now you're taking off with the homeless girl instead!"

Zachary set his lips in a hard line. "In our custodial arrangement, I'll pay for Ashley's education. You can afford the rest of Ashley's expenses if you're careful with your money. Ashley will come to America as soon as her term ends for one month every summer without fail. That's non-negotiable."

"Great plan, Zachary," I affirmed. "With your firm but loving discipline and competent, professional counseling we can help Ashley be less self-focused and cold." I didn't add "like her mother" but it was in my thoughts.

My phone rang. I let it go to voice mail, then checked the message.

Turning to Zachary I said, "Lydia called. She couldn't reach you on your cell. She wants you to return her call no matter what time."

"Thanks. She'll be thrilled with this news."

Laura Anne's face had become the color of paste, but she reluctantly signed the papers that Nick produced. I sighed with relief. If Laura Anne wanted to get off a sarcastic comment, she was interrupted by the inspector who entered from behind the French doors where he'd been listening. I'd called him earlier.

"It could be worse, Mrs. Wycham. You could be going to prison," he announced coldly. "Now at least your husband's motive for taking his own life is clear. You'll excuse me now, I'm leaving to write up my report."

"Get Lizzie here immediately and don't tell her anything yet," Zachary ordered Laura Anne. "I want to handle this myself."

The sweet little girl arrived by cab a few hours later.

Lizzie sat in front of Zachary hesitantly while he held her hand. He gave Lizzie a full explanation. Then she threw her arms around him and he pulled her into his lap.

Lizzie sobbed. "Does this mean I can call you Daddy? I always wanted a Daddy."

"Yes, my dear girl, we'll proceed immediately with your adoption. You're going to be my precious daughter forever. And Ashley will visit us every summer."

EPILOGUE

On the airplane flight back to the States I thought about my amazing husband and the special relationship we have. I suppose it's rather natural to ponder this after being with Laura Anne, a woman who trivialized her vows and Duke George who tried to frame his wife for his death. I thank God every day for blessing me with my husband Nick who's solidly committed to me. Even when I focus extra attention on client's crises, he understands and keeps me covered spiritually with prayer.

I snuggled up next to him best I could on the narrow plane seats. "Nick, do you know how much I appreciate you?" I whispered. "Keeping our marriage commitment is a huge gift we give each other every day."

Nick burrowed his head in my neck. "That's right. I need a lifetime to study you."

Back home in the States, Collin and Tara displayed a burst of enthusiasm over our return. Their excitement lasted a few days. Soon our presence was old news. No matter. Being united as a family is a warm, comfy feeling I will never cease to love.

Lizzie is the luckiest girl in Chicago and, best of all, she's sweet and appreciative. Jenny and I went dress shopping with her and Lydia. Lizzie will be the junior bridesmaid at Lydia and Zachary's wedding next month. Zachary has promised Nick shrimp the size of baby's fists on the hors d'oeuvres table in honor of their friendship.

Zachary exaggerates my sleuthing ability to anyone who will listen. He's very kind, but I'm humbly aware I simply used logic. Plus prayer to the amazing Holy Spirit Who indwells every Christian and is a constant source of wisdom.

For now, I'm fully content to be a happy mom, part-time marriage and family counselor and busy homemaker.

After being in England, the country of famous literary detectives like Sherlock Holmes, Miss Marple and Lord Peter Wimsey, I admit I like solving mysteries even more. If another one appears on my doorstep, well, I won't turn it down.

OTHER BOOKS BY JUDITH ROLFS

MYSTERY AND SUSPENSE:

The Windemere Affair
Bullet in the Night
Never Tomorrow
Directive 99

MARRIAGE & FAMILY:

Man in Command, 52 Ways To Be A Great Husband and Dad
Loving Every Minute, 52 Ways To Live, Laugh & Love As A Woman
Love Always, Mom, a Family Miracle Story
Triumphing Over Cancer Plus 40 Survival Strategies You Can Use

CHILDREN:

Tommy Smurlee and Dunster's Camp of Mystery and Inventions
Tommy Smurlee and the Missing Statue
Mystery of the Silver Shells
Unforgettable Stories For Kids
Hey, I've Got AD(H)D, Here's How You Can Help

DEVOTIONALS:

Jesus Time, Love Notes of Wonder and Worship

God's Near
Joyful Christmas Reflections
God Moments

Available through amazon and local bookstores.

Favorite Scripture Verse: Habakkuk 2:2 "Write the vision and make it plain, that those who run may read it."

ACKNOWLEDGMENTS

I'm blessed to have a number of family members and friends with great literary instincts to consult on my writing journey. Their encouragement and help was invaluable in bringing *Mystery at Wycham Manor* to print. I offer deep appreciation to Pam Ostrander, Dan and Stephanie Rolfs, Becky Melby, Elizabeth Daghfal, Dick Carlson, Delores Leisner. They were my early readers, editors and cheerleaders. This first draft was set aside half-written several years ago. Without the kind words and encouragement of you, my readers, this, my fifth novel, would not have been completed. My husband and I designed the original plot and to honor him I wanted to finish this. Our travels through England and Scotland and the gracious people we met there inspired me to choose this location as a setting for Wycham Manor. My love and gratitude to everyone in my family who has helped me keep moving forward without my husband Wayne, the love of my life. I pray for you all every single day.

ABOUT THE AUTHOR

Dr. Judith Rolfs has over twenty-five fiction and non-fiction books for adults and children. Also a marriage and family therapist, she says, "I like to take readers deep into psychological motivation of my characters and positively influence readers' lives. Mine are old-fashioned mysteries with lots of suspects and twists to challenge readers."

www.judithrolfs.com

Judith Rolfs YouTube channel.

Made in the USA
Columbia, SC
13 February 2025

53716712R00135